LOVE TIMES THREE
Golden Gate Romance Series, Book Four

BARBARA MCMAHON

Love Times Three
Copyright © 2023 Barbara McMahon
All Rights Reserved

1

Asher Callahan took a deep breath as the elevator doors slid open. Stepping into the large open office filled with workstations and desks, he looked straight ahead, toward his private office in the far corner.

For a moment he wished he'd postponed this. His briefcase gripped in one hand, he began the long walk, ignoring the heads that turned his way.

"Sorry about Mrs. Callahan," Joshua called from his station.

Mavis Jones stood as he passed her desk, her features serious and sad.

"I'm so sorry, Asher," she said softly.

He nodded grimly and kept walking. Still dazed by the turn of events, he longed for the sanctity of his office.

It was hard to believe Addie was dead. He didn't realize people still died from pneumonia these days. With all the fancy medicines in the world, they couldn't have stopped the devastation of such an old disease?

"Asher, are you all right?" Sarah Stephens, his secretary, rose from her desk outside his door and moved toward him.

Her eyes brimmed with sympathy.

Asher nodded.

"It was a hellacious trip, but at least I'm home now. How

are things here?"

He clenched his jaw, feeling the strain. It wouldn't get easier any time soon.

"Morale's down. But with the rapid expansion over the last four years, only the old-timers actually knew Addie. Still, many of the employees have talked to her on the phone, and everyone knew she was the other partner."

Noticing she'd avoided the obvious, that Addie had also been his wife, Asher wearily pushed open the door and entered his office.

Mail was stacked in neat piles on the right side of his desk. A small mound of folders sat on the far left side. Pink phone messages were centered with a long cream-colored envelope across them.

He rounded the desk and dropped his briefcase on the credenza behind his chair. The view of San Francisco Bay sparkling in the afternoon sunshine went unnoticed as he surveyed the work waiting.

He was so tired!

"Did you just get in?" Sarah asked, hovering in the doorway.

"The flight finally landed about an hour ago. I came straight here."

"Are you really okay? I know you and Addie lived three thousand miles apart these last three years, but she was your wife."

He glanced at her.

"You know that was a legal technicality." He paused. "Is the gossip mill humming?"

"No more than usual. Those of us who have been here

since the beginning made sure the others knew you and Addie had been married purely to facilitate the start-up of Callahan Associates. I think some of the new employees didn't realize she was your wife. They never met her. She stayed in New York, as you know."

He nodded. He skimmed the top message, then flicked the envelope.

"What's this?"

The rest of his mail had been opened and lay in one of his folders.

"I separated those messages. They've been calling every day for the last two weeks. Yesterday we received the registered letter. I tried to explain why we couldn't reach you in Bangkok. Obviously they weren't monitoring the news or they would have heard about the typhoon."

Asher shrugged. He slipped out of his suit jacket, draped it across the back of his chair and slowly sat.

"Anyone from here attend the funeral?" he asked.

"No. But most of the New York office went. Bob Mason sent a report. I put it in the folder with the rest of your mail. Don't blame yourself for not being there, Asher. You would have been there had it been possible. Addie would have understood."

"Why are these lawyers calling?"

Asher didn't want to review why he hadn't been able to get to New York in time. He'd tried his best, but fate had decreed otherwise. It was over and done with, time to move on.

His anger at fate had abated, and a philosophical calm replaced it. If anyone had understood business problems, it had been Addie. She'd thrived on them.

"They didn't tell me, just insisted they had to reach you. I gave them the Bangkok telephone number, so they could see for themselves why we couldn't get through. You know lawyers—not very trusting. Why they'd think we were trying to hinder communications, I don't know."

"Thanks, Sarah."

"Let me know if you need anything."

"Right."

She eased the door almost shut as Asher picked up the envelope. He was dead tired. Flying through more than half a dozen time zones did that—especially after two weeks of hell. If he were a superstitious man, he'd be convinced the deal he was working on was jinxed.

The trip had started off wrong, with mechanical difficulties on the outbound airplane forcing an emergency stop on Wake Island. Then there'd been the wild, bumpy flight into Bangkok, followed by a customs mix up.

Bad weather plagued him from the moment he left the airport.

The hotel where he had reservations had burned the night before his arrival, and he'd had to locate new lodgings before the predicted typhoon hit. He'd barely informed his office of the change in location before the high winds and torrential rains of Typhoon Initi let loose.

Severe storms did major damage in the United States, but recovery time was usually rapid. In Bangkok, it seemed interminable. He'd received word of Addie's death only hours before the full force of the typhoon hit.

Airplanes had been grounded, communications and

electricity cut off due to high winds.

The streets flooded. Accidents abounded.

It had been days before a semblance of normal activities resumed.

Days before he could contact his office to notify them he'd return on the first available flight.

Asher tapped the edge of the envelope on the desk, wishing he could quantify his feelings about Addie's death. He shook his head, feeling vaguely impatient.

They'd been married for more than six years. Even though their marriage had been primarily a business arrangement she'd been a friend and one-time lover. Maybe fatigue numbed his reactions, dulled his emotions. He had trouble picturing the world without her sharp wit and dogged determination to build the biggest and best.

Shock had been replaced with disbelief. She was twenty-nine—too young to die. Especially with all she wanted to accomplish so close to being achieved.

He hadn't seen her in over a year—and that had been when they'd met in Washington, D.C., with the congressmen from California for the discussion of Pacific Rim trade regulations.

But they talked on the phone frequently, kept in touch by e-mail, texts and Zoom.

Married six years, separated by a continent for the last three of those years, it hadn't been much of a relationship.

Except in business—Addie shone in that arena. It had been her idea to expand into the European market. She'd insisted she be the one to move to New York to set up that office.

From the initial discussion to her transfer things had moved like a whirlwind.

Once she left San Francisco, she never looked back—never came back, even for a flying visit.

And he hadn't missed her. Their electronic connection had been enough.

Now he'd miss her, if only in business.

Asher sighed and slit open the envelope. Slowly he began to read.

Stunned, he reread the letter.

Unbelievable!

"Sarah," he roared.

He read the words a third time. Was this some kind of joke? How could—

"Sarah!"

The door opened slightly. Asher looked into the diffident gaze of Charlotte Thompson. His mind occupied with the contents of the letter, it took him a moment to register it wasn't Sarah warily watching him.

"Sorry, Asher, Sarah stepped away from her desk. Can I help you?"

"Read this and tell me what it says."

Asher stood and thrust out the letter.

Charlotte entered the office, carrying a thin manila folder in one hand. She'd been lurking outside his door on the off chance Asher would have a few minutes in which she could discuss the World vision merger.

When she'd heard him call Sarah, she'd looked for the secretary. When he'd called again, she felt someone should respond.

She crossed the expanse of his office and gingerly took the paper.

Asher ran his fingers through his hair as he studied her.

Charlotte dropped her gaze to the typed letter.

She'd started with Callahan Associates two years ago, immediately after graduating from the MBA program at Berkeley. However, her interaction with the senior partner had been minimal. After all, he was the head of the firm, one of the two partners, and she a mere marketing analyst.

She looked at him, puzzled, unsure why he wanted her to read the letter.

"It seems the attorneys in New York are wondering when you will be coming to get your twin daughters."

Was she supposed to deduce something else from the letter?

Asher sat down, staring at Charlotte.

"Twins."

Uneasily, Charlotte perched on the edge of a chair and gravely studied him across his desk.

She swallowing visibly, then said, "It, um, almost sounds as if you were unaware of their existence."

"I had no idea."

How could Addie give birth to his daughters and not tell him?

Charlotte said nothing. Gently she laid the letter on his desk.

Asher rifled through the pink telephone slips. Each one from the same people—Addie's attorneys in New York. Slowly he picked up one and punched in the number.

It rang endlessly.

"It's after five in New York," Charlotte said softly.

Slipping the receiver on the cradle, Asher nodded. The last thing he expected today was to discover he was a father. Or was he?

Why hadn't Addie told him if he were the father?

"You needed me, boss?" Sarah asked from the doorway.

"Are you *sure* none of these lawyers told you why they were calling?" Asher asked, flicking an impatient finger against the stack of phone messages.

She nodded.

"Read this."

He tossed her the letter.

Sarah glanced at Charlotte as she crossed to take the letter. Reading it, her eyes widened with surprise.

"Wow, congratulations, Asher. You're a daddy."

"You think so?"

She looked puzzled. "It says so."

"You know that Addie moved east almost three years ago to open the New York office. Unless she was pregnant when she left, those children aren't mine."

Sarah glanced again at Charlotte.

"Maybe you better wait and talk about this later. After you talk to the attorneys."

"I tried them, they didn't answer. It's late in New York. I'll call in the morning."

"Or try one of them at home," Charlotte offered.

Asher looked at her.

"Good idea. See if you can find home numbers for any of the partners," Asher directed Sarah.

When Sarah left, Charlotte rose tentatively, holding out

the manila folder to Asher.

"You probably don't want to be bothered with this right now, but these are the projections we did for the World vision account. I'm confident they're solid, a bit ambitious but achievable. If anything, we erred on the conservative side."

Asher took the folder and leaned back in his chair.

Petite, with glossy black hair, Charlotte represented the epitome of the young executive on the rise. She always wore her dark hair in a conservative French braid, tidy, neat, severe.

Dark-framed glasses perched on her nose. Irreverently Asher thought they made her look like an owl, trying unsuccessfully to hide her eyes. Large and dark, fringed with long lashes, they were her best feature.

Asher idly let his gaze drift down her neat suit, navy blue with a standard white blouse. The perfect business-woman— all work-oriented with femininity ruthlessly squashed.

Just like Addie.

Was she as ambitious? As consumed with work?

He took the papers and skimmed the top sheet, but his mind wasn't on the figures.

Twins.

He felt stunned. Could it be possible? Had Addie been pregnant when she left San Francisco?

If so, why had she kept the news from him?

He couldn't believe it. Yet the attorney's letter seemed clear on the subject.

"We're all sorry about Mrs. Callahan's death," Charlotte said.

Meeting her eyes, Asher stared at her for a long moment. How was he to answer the sentiment? The employees probably expected a grieving husband.

Sarah said they understood his marriage. He mourned the loss of a close friend, a strong business associate.

Yet now it looked as if he hadn't known Addie like he'd thought.

What was the story with the twins?

"Thank you," he said.

What he'd like to do was go home, pour himself a large Scotch and sleep for twelve hours. Instead, he'd wait to see if Sarah could reach someone from the New York law office so he could find out what the hell was going on.

"Line one," Sarah's voice came on the intercom. "Mr. Randall."

"Asher Callahan here," he said into the phone, motioning Charlotte to sit down again.

"We've been trying to reach you for over a week, Callahan."

The speaker had a definite New York accent.

"I believe my secretary explained where I was. The airport just reopened in Bangkok. I actually was on one of the first flights out."

"Are you now back in the States?"

"As of a couple of hours ago. I arrived at the office and found your letter. What kind of scam is this?"

As far as Asher was concerned, it was exactly that unless proved otherwise.

"No scam, Callahan. Madison and Kennedy Callahan are your daughters, twins. Cute as can be, too."

"I never heard about them."

He glanced at Charlotte, noticing her downcast eyes, as if

she were trying to efface her existence. Discreet.

There was a hesitation on the other end of the line.

"I am aware of that. Apparently Mrs. Callahan was concerned that you would insist on someone else being in charge of the New York office if you discovered the truth. She, er, enjoyed the business aspect of things—apparently had no inclination to give it up for full-time motherhood. Not that she wasn't a fine mother."

Sounded like lawyer talk—covering all bases, Asher thought

He closed his eyes. Addie had been right. He'd have moved heaven and earth to keep her in San Francisco if he'd known she was pregnant. And probably demanded she curtail some of her activities at the office.

A mother's place was with her children at least when they were babies.

"How old are they?" Asher asked, a sinking feeling in his gut.

Could they truly be his? Had Addie hidden that from him just to make sure she could keep forging ahead in the business world? Given her unrelenting determination, he could easily imagine her doing that.

"Two. A month or so over, maybe. I have the file at the office. I can look up their birth date in the morning, if you like. Mrs. Callahan made it clear that they were yours and she had not told you of their birth. We thought you'd be here for the funeral and the reading of the will. Actually, we haven't read the will yet. Two-year-olds don't understand much, and she left everything she had to them, with you as trustee. We can go over all that when you get here."

"And where are the twins now?" Asher asked, the enormity of the situation gradually sinking in.

He was a father. He had two daughters he'd never met who now would looked to him for everything.

Good grief, he knew nothing about being a parent.

He focused on Charlotte, feeling like she was the only solid, real thing in a world suddenly spinning out of control. Her calm demeanor soothed him. Her downcast eyes had him wondering what she was thinking.

"We didn't want them to go into foster care, so one of the receptionists at the office agreed to watch them. She has children of her own and is good with kids. But this has gone on longer than we anticipated."

"I'll see if I can get a red-eye tonight and be in your office first thing in the morning." Asher hung up the phone.

"I'll call the airlines right away," Sarah said from the doorway.

"You heard?" he asked.

"Enough to know you have to get back there. Are the twins yours?"

"Apparently. The age fits. Addie told him they were mine. She left everything to them with me as trustee. Blast it all! What a mess. I can't believe she didn't tell me."

"Well, I can. Would you have gone along with her opening a branch office if you'd known?" Sarah asked dryly.

Shaking his head, Asher looked at her.

"What do I know about twins? About little kids?"

He rubbed his eyes, his gut churning.

"For one thing, you'll need someone to accompany you," Charlotte said.

She knew a lot about children, more than she wanted.

"Toddlers are a handful. An inexperienced person would be hard-pressed to manage one on a plane—much less twins. Those little girls will be upset with all the changes, and probably missing their mother, which could make them even more fretful."

Both Asher and Sarah stared at her.

"I assumed you'll be bringing them home with you," Charlotte said, looking from one to the other.

"If they're mine, I'll have no choice."

Charlotte nodded. Twins. She smiled gently. She remembered the little boys she'd cared for when she'd been sixteen. What imps they'd been. Whether from being twins or being normal rambunctious boys, she never knew. But they sure kept her busy.

"Any other words of wisdom?" Asher asked.

She gave a small shrug.

"I've been around kids. If you haven't, you might not know what to expect."

Asher couldn't believe it. This epitome of a career-track businesswoman around kids? She wasn't married, was she? He tried to remember the interview two years ago. He had been more interested in her credentials than her marital status. But he was certain she was single.

"When were you around kids, in another life?"

She nodded. A life she had hoped to leave behind once she graduated from college. The past two years had been great, no children demanding attention or to fall for and then have to give up. She had her way to make in the world and relished her position at Callahan Associates.

Children didn't figure in her plans.

"She's right, Asher. You'll need help. You would with even a single child," Sarah said. "I'll see if I can find someone to go with you. You'll need to hire a nanny or housekeeper, though it's quite late to get anyone on such short notice."

"Do the best you can. And see what kind of nonstop flight you can get to New York tonight."

Charlotte rose.

"Do you want to hear my recommendations on World vision while you're waiting? I could get started on some of the ideas while you're in New York, if you approve."

Business first, last and always, Asher thought tightly. Just like Addie.

"Show me what you have."

He spread out the computer printout and began to read.

Forty-five minutes later Asher leaned back. He rubbed his eyes with forefinger and thumb, then stretched to get rid of the kinks in his back. That Scotch sounded better and better.

The work Charlotte had done was solid, just as she'd said. Interestingly, she gave credit to the entire team she headed, but he knew everyone acted under her direction. She was good at her job—he'd suspected she would be when he hired her two years ago, nearly a year after Addie had moved to New York.

The twins would have been born around the time Charlotte started at the company.

"So we go?" she asked, a tremor of excitement in her voice, a hint of anticipation in her eyes.

"We go. Good job."

He believed in giving praise where it was due.

She smiled. Asher felt the jolt to his toes. Her face seemed to glow with the offhand praise. Her eyes sparkled, and for the first time he wondered what she would look like without her glasses. What would she look like with her hair down, swirling softly around her face? What would she look like wearing something frilly and feminine?

Before he could pursue the image, Sarah stuck her head in.

"Got you two seats on the eleven-thirty flight tonight. And four seats on a return flight tomorrow. But no help as of yet. Every agency I called said they'd look into it. One called back with a possible for next week. Nothing for today. And they're closing now, so I don't expect any answers before tomorrow."

"So what next?" Asher murmured, his eyes closed.

He longed for that Scotch more than ever. Maybe he'd have time to get home, shower and have one before he had to leave for the airport.

How much work did he absolutely have to get through before leaving?

His employees were competent. He could delegate everything until he returned from New York.

The looming problem with the twins overshadowed normal business issues.

"Maybe Charlotte can go with you. She said she knows kids," Sarah suggested.

"What?"

Charlotte shook her head, a look of sheer horror on her face.

"No way. I swore once I grew up I'd never get involved baby-sitting children again. I don't want to spend even an hour watching other people's kids."

Asher and Sarah stared at her vehemence.

She took a deep breath, knowing she'd overreacted. But she was adamant—she had watched her last child.

She was a businesswoman. Hadn't Asher just praised her work? Given her the go-ahead on the World vision project?

She had better things to do than baby-sit the boss's children.

"You wouldn't be watching them, precisely," Sarah said placatingly. "Just helping Asher with them on the return flight. He needs your expertise."

Charlotte shook her head. The old feeling of helplessness began to rise.

Why did everyone expect her to be the nurturer? What about her *own* needs? When would someone look to see what *she* wanted, needed, to feel complete? To feel valued?

She was more than a competent baby-sitter—and had the degrees to prove it.

Asher narrowed his eyes.

"Sounds like the best suggestion I've heard so far. It'll just be a short jaunt to New York. We'll discuss World vision on the flight over. You can give me pointers on watching twins on the flight back. Consider it part of your job."

"It's not part of my job."

Charlotte faced him, her hands fisted. She dare not cross

the line with her boss, but she had to stand up for herself. She didn't want to be thought of as a nanny for children just because she was a woman.

For a moment Asher was struck by the sparkle in her dark eyes, the challenging tilt of her rounded chin.

Slowly he said, "There's a clause in your job description that includes other tasks as assigned. I need help, doesn't look like anyone else is available. As of now, consider this as another task assigned."

"You're his secretary, can't you go?" Charlotte turned to Sarah, her plea obvious.

"Afraid not. I have an invalid mother I care for. I can't leave her alone overnight. Besides, I don't know any more about children than Asher."

"I was hired as a marketing analyst, not a nanny," Charlotte protested, swinging to Asher.

Frustration and fatigue edged him.

"I believe in utilizing all experiences of my employees. Consider yourself indispensable for this assignment."

"I protest." She said it firmly, yet deep inside she knew it wouldn't matter. Asher wasn't listening.

"It's settled. Meet me at the airport in time for the flight. Sarah, give her the details. I'm heading home."

He caught her eye and narrowed his. "Don't be late!"

Charlotte watched him leave, the unfairness of it all striking her. She met the sympathy in Sarah's gaze.

"He needs your help. You said you know something about kids, he hasn't a clue. It's just overnight, Charlotte," the older woman said.

"I'm always the one stuck with children. For years, it was always, 'Leave them with Charlotte'. Working here was my chance to leave that behind," she said wryly, rising. "Guess that was wishful thinking."

She took a deep breath. Trying to look on the bright side of things, she returned to her desk. Casting her mind back, she tried to picture the needs and abilities of toddlers. It really hadn't been that long since she'd been in charge of little children. She could certainly handle a cross-country flight.

And she'd have Asher's attention on the flight to New York. Maybe she could discuss some of her other ideas with him.

Looking for the silver lining, she swept folders into her briefcase and headed home to pack.

Four hours later Asher leaned back on his sofa watching the clock on the mantel. In ten minutes he had to leave for the airport. He'd had a Scotch, but it had done nothing to ease the turmoil.

Sleeping had been out of the question—he'd been afraid he wouldn't wake up in time for the flight. He'd sleep on the plane. It'd have to do.

He considered the situation once again, trying to make some sense of it.

Oddly, his thoughts kept returning to Charlotte Thompson. For the two years she'd worked for him, he'd barely noticed her. She'd done her job well, already had one promotion behind her. Recently she'd been assigned as project manager for the World vision account. Accomplished, proficient, professional—all desirable attributes for a career-minded woman.

Her surprising outburst this afternoon startled him. Asher liked things to make sense, to follow a logical pattern—and that hadn't.

She was usually enthusiastic and agreeable, and her refusal had been surprising and unusual. A mere suggestion to accompany him on the trip to see to the children, help bring them to San Francisco, and she'd about exploded.

He wondered why.

Maybe he'd discover on the trip.

The red-eye flight would arrive in New York just after eight. They'd go directly to the attorney's office upon landing. Asher had showered and shaved, donned a fresh suit and shirt. His overnight case contained casual clothes for the return journey. He might not know much about children, but he knew enough to suspect they'd be too messy for an Armani suit.

He wondered what he should be taking to entertain two toddlers.

His thoughts veered to the babies. How could Addie have kept them a secret? If her lawyer was to be believed, she feared he'd demand she return to San Francisco.

Would that have been so bad? They'd worked together at McGeorge and Fergerson, discussed starting a business for months before taking the plunge. She'd been as much invested in the company as he.

Pouring all their resources into the firm, they'd conserved

on expenses by marrying each other. He liked the challenge of building a company, but sometimes he thought Addie defined herself by the company and its success.

Had business been more important to her than her children? Their children?

He rose, not liking the trend of his thoughts. He grabbed the overnight case and started for the airport.

Charlotte sat alone in a bank of chairs at the boarding gate, casually leafing through a magazine, a small tote bag beside her feet.

She might resent the assignment, but she was professional enough to do her best. Knowing they'd head directly for the attorney's offices, she'd dressed in a charcoal gray suit matched with a white blouse. Both traveled well, and she hoped she wouldn't look like a wrinkled mess in the morning.

A tingling awareness struck her, and she raised her gaze. As if attuned to him, she spotted her boss as he crossed the concourse toward the gate.

She sighed softly and sat up straighter. Asher was so good-looking he shouldn't be let out without a keeper.

She noticed the glances he received from the other women in the area. Some bold and interested, others more surreptitious, but all following his long stride as he crossed to join her. His dark hair was thick and neatly trimmed. The tan he'd had in the summer wasn't as evident after his recent trip, but the rugged masculinity in his face struck a spark of interest for the first time.

Charlotte frowned. Was it knowing he was single again

that caused that?

She'd thought he was drop-dead gorgeous when he'd interviewed her, but so far out of her league, she'd immediately ignored the sensations that fluttered inside and concentrated on doing the best she could on her assignments.

In reality, nothing had changed. So why this sudden awareness?

She smiled politely as he drew closer.

"Here as ordered, sir," she said briefly.

He sat beside her and glanced at her carry on bag and briefcase. A sardonic smile creased his cheeks.

"You sound like a kitten spitting at a bulldog. Just remember who's the boss."

She met his hard eyes, a faint hint of anger visible in her gaze.

"No danger of forgetting that, is there, sir?"

Asher smiled.

She tightened her lips and returned to her magazine before she gave way to the urge to wipe that smug grin off his face.

"Do you sleep in suits?" he asked.

"What?"

She looked around and stared at him in disbelief.

"Just wondering. Addie wore suits all the time except to bed. I thought you might wear something more comfortable for the flight."

"This is appropriate attire for a business meeting. We *are* meeting the lawyers before we see your daughters, right?" she replied.

"Maybe they'll be dressed like miniature businesswomen,

too," he murmured, not putting it past Addie.

Wearily Asher felt as if he'd never known his wife at all.

"I doubt it." She eyed his suit. "I hope *you* brought something else. Kids can be messy, especially when confined in airplanes."

He looked at her lazily.

"I have a couple of changes in the bag. I figured we would stay at least one night in New York. If I don't get some sleep soon, I'm going to pass out."

He rubbed his eyes with his thumb and forefinger.

"You can sleep on the plane. Didn't Sarah said she booked return tickets for tomorrow?"

Compassion struck Charlotte. He looked exhausted. After flying in from Asia, it had to be next to impossible to fly on to New York.

"I don't even remember. After the flight from Bangkok and the flight tonight, my body won't know whether it's coming or going. Do you know how many time zones I've crossed in the last twenty-four hours?"

She shook her head, her gaze moving slowly over his shoulders to the long legs stretched out before him. So much for her idea of discussing business on the flight to New York. She hoped he'd stay awake to get to his seat on the plane.

For a moment Charlotte wondered what it would be like to travel with him when he was rested. Would he be a fascinating conversationalist? He'd been to so many places and done so much. Wasn't he only in his early thirties? She'd love to hear how he and his wife had started Callahan Associates and where they planned to take the company.

But it wasn't going to happen tonight.

Asher idly noted Charlotte's perusal. Or was he imagining it?

She probably wanted to discuss the bottom line or future projections and was trying to think up the best approach. She was no more interested in him than he was in her.

And he was not interested in anyone at the moment.

Except he couldn't quite explain the desire to loosen her dark hair, unbutton that high collar and remove the glasses. He couldn't remember if he'd ever seen her not wearing them. He wouldn't mind seeing her in a dress, or shorts—or nothing at all.

Nothing?

Man, he must be tired—now he was hallucinating. Closing his eyes, he tried to focus on the impending meeting with his daughters. Disbelief warred with fascination. He had no time for idle fantasies about one of his employees—one, moreover, who reminded him strongly of his late wife.

He'd had his fill of determined career women who cared more for competing in the business world than in making a home and planning a future complete with family.

Next time he ventured into a personal relationship, he'd find someone soft and feminine and more interested in flowers in the garden and a comfortable home than spreadsheets and bank statements and projected earnings.

That's what he'd look for—if he ever wanted to marry again.

The flight was called.

Asher and Charlotte boarded first class. He offered her the window seat.

"I plan to sleep the entire trip so I don't need to see out

the window," he said.

"Thank you. Though I should mention I'll also be napping. If not, I'll be a zombie tomorrow."

She slipped in, stowed her bag and briefcase, clutched her magazine like a lifeline.

Bemused, Charlotte realized she could smell his after-shave lotion—tangy and masculine.

Sitting close enough to feel the heat from his strong body, she wanted to draw away, but there was only the airplane wall on the other side. Tongue-tied and feeling awkward, she gazed at the magazine, wondering why all her common sense seemed to have gone cockeyed.

Asher sat beside her, fastening his seat belt. She'd attended meetings in the conference room that he'd chaired. So what was the problem tonight?

Of course, at the meetings, she hadn't sat beside him. Not been so acutely aware of his strong hands, the width of his shoulders and the smooth skin of his freshly shaved jaw. She tightened her grip lest her fingers give way to the desire to brush against that stubborn jaw and test the texture of his skin, feel his heat on her fingertips.

Charlotte swallowed hard, moving her gaze out the window. There was little to see in the darkness. Lights lit the service vehicles scurrying around the big jet, but beyond that nothing was visible. Yet she continued to stare out the window. It felt safer, somehow.

"As soon as we get airborne, I'm reclining the seat and going to sleep. If anyone asks, I don't want food or drink," he murmured in her right ear.

Charlotte turned and drew in her breath. His face was

mere inches from hers. She could see the lines of fatigue radiating from his eyes and her own image reflected there. His breath caressed her cheek. Swallowing, she nodded, fascinated to be so close to the man.

"Been to New York before?" he asked, his eyes searching hers.

She shook her head, conscious of the wild beat of her heart. Mesmerized by the sensations that raced through her, she couldn't look away.

"Sorry we won't have time to go sight-seeing."

"I hope to go one day on vacation. I'd like to see the sights, maybe go to a Broadway show."

"It's okay to visit, but I prefer San Francisco any day."

Charlotte nodded.

"Are you from the Bay Area?" he asked.

She shook her head. Feeling like an idiot and not the competent woman she tried to portray, she cleared her throat.

"I grew up near L.A. Now I prefer San Francisco."

"Live in the city?"

"In a small place on Telegraph Hill."

"Lots of tourists."

"Mostly in the summer. Coit Tower is a popular site. I like to walk up there myself and gaze out over the city. It offers magnificent views."

"How long have you lived there?" Asher asked, wondering why he didn't know more about an employee who had worked for him for two years.

"I moved in a couple of weeks before I went to work for you," she replied.

Why didn't he lean back in his seat? Why was he still so

close, close enough for her to feel as if there were only the two of them on the entire plane? She longed for some distance. His eyes were dark, compelling, mesmerizing. She liked the lights that danced in their depth. Wondered what he thought as he gazed into her eyes.

The flight attendant began her preflight demonstration. Charlotte drew a deep breath and looked at the woman. She knew Asher continued to watch her through narrowed eyes, but she focused on the demonstration as if she'd never seen one before. Almost feeling the waves of fatigue wash through him, she knew he'd last only a few more minutes. Once he reclined his seat and slept, the trip would be easier.

Asher awoke as the plane began its descent. He felt the pressure in his ears and yawned to relieve it.

Something heavy and warm rested against his shoulder. Turning his head, he realized Charlotte had decided to use him as a pillow during the night. Both of them were covered with airline blankets. Both seats had been reclined. Had he done this? Had she?

He shifted a bit, his arm asleep. How long had she rested against him? A faint hint of roses wafted on the air. Her special scent? He tipped his face toward her and took a breath. Sweet, definitely roses.

Closing his eyes, he tried to envision her purchasing that particular scent and spraying it on each morning. Somehow it evoked images of a different woman, soft and feminine—not a straitlaced, ambitious businesswoman.

He had to get a grip. She wasn't there to be his personal fantasy, but to play nanny to his daughters on the return trip. That was all. Once they reached San Francisco, she'd resume her role as marketing analyst, and Sarah would have located a nanny for the twins. He had other things to think about besides Charlotte Thompson.

Immediately thoughts of the twins had him awake and alert.

He shook his seat companion, then waited while she slowly came awake.

"Oh, sorry."

Instantly she pushed back and sat up. Her cheek was warm and rosy, with a slight crease mark from his jacket crossing it diagonally. She looked at him and blinked. The glasses were gone. Her eyes were dark and mysterious.

Slowly Asher felt attraction build.

Glasses off, she looked younger, shy almost, and definitely as feminine as he could ever wish. Her tight French braid had worked loose during the night. Wispy tendrils of glossy dark hair framed her face. When she licked dry lips, he felt a sharp tug of awareness—total male awareness of an attractive female.

All thoughts of sleep fled. Suddenly he was more than curious about this woman.

"I didn't mean to fall asleep on you," she said, moving farther away, straightening her clothes beneath the blanket, retrieving her glasses.

Asher experienced a repeat urge to unbutton the top of her blouse to enable more of her warmth and sweet scent to fill his senses. He looked at her moist lips and yearned to taste them.

Closing his eyes, he turned away. He'd been too long without a woman. Even in a business marriage, he'd believed in keeping his vows. Since Addie had departed almost three years ago, he'd spent his nights alone.

Sexual deprivation—that was all it was. And now that his wife was dead, he was free to consider other women. Nothing more than that.

He wasn't attracted to Charlotte. Any woman would affect him the same way.

Opening his eyes, he didn't bother to analyze why there was no pull of attraction between him and the buxom blond flight attendant. Instead, he tried to ignore the attraction to the woman beside him and concentrate on attempting to anticipate the information he'd receive from the attorney.

When they landed, Asher reached for Charlotte's cases and carried them easily.

"I can manage my own cases," she protested, following him up the jetway.

"I don't mind. You'll have your hands full later. No sense in not taking advantage of my generous nature now."

"Generous, my foot," she mumbled. "Dictatorial, more likely."

"Why's that?" Asher found himself amused at her grumbling.

Was she always cranky in the morning? For the first time her perfect image shifted, blurred. He liked her better when she wasn't the flawless employee.

"You ordered me here. I didn't want to come."

"Don't you like children?"

"I don't like watching them."

"When was the last time you did?"

Kennedy Airport hummed with activity. A uniformed

man stood in the crowd holding Asher's name on a card. Asher handed the limousine driver the bags. Following him, Asher placed his hand on Charlotte's back. She was not as tall as Addie had been. Yet she held her head high and marched determinedly after the driver.

"Children?" Asher said again, a hint of steel in his voice.

"I've had to watch children almost all my life. I swore when I was on my own I wouldn't do it again. I'm not real happy with this assignment. If you hadn't made it an order, I wouldn't be here," she grumbled.

Despite her annoyance with her high-handed boss, she was fascinated with the bustle of the international airport.

"Ah, but think of the brownie points you can rack up helping the boss out this way."

"I'd rather get points for merit than for baby-sitting capability."

"Maybe the merit is in the baby-sitting," he replied calmly, noting her agitation. "Tell me about watching kids all your life."

"I'd rather not. I'm sorry I opened my mouth yesterday."

"About knowing about twins?"

She nodded. Dodging a man obviously in a hurry to make a plane, she pushed against Asher. He shifted her to the other side, continued walking smoothly.

"It slipped out," she said.

More curious than ever, Asher wondered if he could get the full story from her before they met with Addie's attorneys.

2

"I have to compliment you on your restraint and tact," Asher said to Charlotte when they were seated in the back of the limousine heading for Manhattan.

"About what?" she asked warily.

After entering the limousine, Charlotte had moved as close to the far door as possible. Asher almost smiled at the distance she placed between them. Was she uncomfortable around him? Interesting. For a moment he considered testing the theory.

"Another woman would have bombarded me with questions about my marriage, my wife and why I apparently have two-year-old daughters I know nothing about," he said instead.

"Of course I'm curious, but I do respect your right to privacy."

She tilted her head and smiled mischievously.

"And I picked up quite a bit from around the office. The scuttlebutt is that you two married to pool resources so you could build Callahan Associates. She moved to New York a few years ago to open a second office and to try to crack the European market. She had two little girls you knew nothing about. If there's more you want to volunteer, I wouldn't interrupt."

Startled, Asher almost laughed aloud at the unexpected glimpse of minx in his companion. He knew what she had told him was no secret—except for the babies. He was more intrigued that she had apparently picked up quite a bit. Any special reason?

"Ours was not an ordinary marriage. We married for expediency. Starting up a new company calls for a lot of hard work, long hours and money. It was easier to minimize expenses and to work long hours by sharing a home."

He wasn't trying to justify the relationship, just explain it. Why that was important, he wasn't sure.

"Sounds like a business arrangement."

"Essentially."

He'd almost forgotten how it started. For the last three years they'd shared nothing beyond a meal in Washington.

"Addie wanted Callahan Associates to succeed even more than I did. She found the business environment challenging and exciting."

"It can be exhilarating," Charlotte murmured, watching him closely.

"I know. Now I understand her sudden determination to move to New York and open an East Coast office. She never came back to San Francisco because she feared she'd be stuck with the babies rather than in the trenches of high-tech business, I think."

"Not every woman wants to stay home and raise children."

"You don't," he stated with certainty.

Her outburst yesterday in his office confirmed that.

"What I want right now is a chance to build a life of my

own. Maybe down the road I'll marry and have children. Then I'll have to see what I want to do. Children are fine as long as they're wanted and loved."

"I hear a but."

"But I don't want the choice taken from me."

"As I did with this assignment?"

She nodded, looking out the window as the tall skyscrapers of Manhattan came into view. Puffy white clouds drifted in azure blue skies. Traffic was heavy, but moved steadily on the congested highway. Asher wondered if her attention was truly taken with the approaching city or if she was trying to distance herself to rebuild her anger. It had blown over quickly. He was glad she wasn't the type to sulk.

"Be honest, Charlotte. I didn't ask for much. A day to help get them home. Sarah is working on finding a nanny. You have experience I lack. Wouldn't you take advantage of any needed expertise?"

"Probably," she admitted grudgingly.

"Where does that expertise come from? Lots of brothers and sisters?"

He knew he was probing where she didn't want him to, but his curiosity rose. Solemn and serious, Charlotte Thompson never gave the impression she was anything but a well-trained employee.

Yet she had to have a private life—he didn't demand his employees dedicate their entire waking hours to the job. Suddenly he wanted to know more.

"None, actually."

"We have about thirty minutes before we arrive at the attorneys' office. Why don't you tell me about your experience with children."

If she wouldn't open up voluntarily, he'd ask specific questions. For a moment he wondered why he pushed. Was it only curiosity, or was he trying to stop thinking about two toddlers waiting to meet him?

He'd negotiated multi million-dollar deals. Why was he growing more and more nervous at the thought of facing two small girls?

The silence stretched. Charlotte slowly turned and looked at him. She didn't like to talk about her past. All her life she'd wished for a fairy-tale family, something like the Brady Bunch—a dream far from her reality.

She guessed it wouldn't hurt to explain why she hadn't wanted to come on this trip.

"My mother died when I was seven. I had no other family, so I ended up in foster care. The home I was assigned when I was ten had lots of young children, mostly other foster kids. I baby-sat constantly over the next eight years. Once I turned eighteen, I split. No more kids for me, I vowed."

"Until today."

"I wish. When I got to college, I needed money. Only job I was qualified for was watching children. So I was a prime candidate for professors' families looking for a nanny. Another four years of watching other people's kids. Once I had my degree, I wanted my MBA. Another year."

"Now my request."

"Right." She frowned. "It's not what I expected when I hired on with the firm. I have a degree in marketing and business, not child care. I want to use my mind, not be a baby-sitter."

"Nor did I ever think I'd need a nanny. But then I had no idea Addie had delivered twins."

Asher lapsed into silence, again wondering how Addie could have kept such an event from him. After all, he couldn't have made her return to San Francisco to live. He *should* have known about his daughters.

The law offices of Sattler, Randall and Peabody were located on the thirty-third floor of a skyscraper on East Fortieth Street. A high-speed elevator whisked them quickly to their destination. Asher located the door to the offices, pushed it open and stood aside to allow Charlotte to enter. Stepping inside, he immediately stopped, his eyes on the two toddlers playing by a maroon-colored crushed velvet sofa. Dark hair caught up in wispy ponytails, matching overalls, a pink shirt and a yellow shirt on the two little girls—other than those shirts, they were identical. Both stopped playing when Asher entered, turning toward him and Charlotte, bright blue eyes staring.

Asher stood more than six feet tall. Did he seem like a giant to these little creatures? They were so tiny. For an instant he stared in fascination, wondering what they thought. Neither said a word, just stared.

"Hello, there."

Charlotte greeted the little girls with a wide smile and moved closer.

They were precious. Her heart went out to them. Things must be so scary. Charlotte remembered how scared she'd been when her mother died and she had gone to live with strangers. Nothing had been familiar, nothing comforting.

And she'd missed her mother so much.

Smiling, she knelt before the girls and slowly reached out to touch each one on her hand. "Hi, I'm Lottie. What are your names?"

Asher heard the warmth and softness in her voice. It broke the spell.

The twins smiled and shifted their gaze to Charlotte. When she knelt before them, they launched into babbling that had Asher's head spinning. Would she understand anything they were saying? He'd forgotten how small two-year-olds were. They didn't even talk well.

"Mr. Callahan?"

The woman behind the reception desk greeted him. Her smile was friendly.

"That's right."

"Cute kids you have," she said with a glance at the twins. "I've been watching them for the last two weeks. They're as sweet as can be. I'm so sorry about your wife."

Asher nodded, feeling totally out of his element. He knew nothing about children—knew nothing about his own daughters.

Fortunately, Charlotte appeared to know all that was needed. The twins took to her like ducks to water. Laughing and talking, the three of them, all the same height with Charlotte kneeling, seemed to mesh perfectly. For a moment Asher was envious. He watched them while the receptionist notified the attorney of Asher's arrival.

"Mr. Randall will be with you in just a moment," the receptionist said, seemingly unaware of his hesitation.

Nodding, Asher moved slowly across the reception area toward his children. One look at them and all doubts fled.

They looked just like he had as a child—though feminine versions. He could see nothing of Addie in either child except for her blue eyes. Had they inherited her temperament or ambition?

"Hello," he said.

Two pairs of identical eyes swiveled to him. The little girl in yellow put her thumb in her mouth, watching him warily.

"I think you are a bit too tall for them. Either pick them up or get down on their level," Charlotte suggested, leaning on her heels.

She brushed the hair off the face of the child sucking her thumb.

Asher stared at the unwavering eyes regarding him. Slowly he sat on the edge of the sofa, totally at a loss. He didn't like the feeling. Over the years, he'd perfected his ability to fit in with different cultures, different societies as he expanded Callahan Associates in Pacific Rim countries.

Now he was floored by a pair of toddlers.

"Smile," Charlotte said, the lilt in her voice one of amusement. She looked at the girls.

"This is your daddy. Tell him your name," she prompted the twin in pink.

"Madsen," she said proudly, her gaze steady.

Popping her thumb from her mouth, the other twin piped up. "Me Kenny."

"Madison and Kennedy," Charlotte repeated, smiling at them. "And this is your daddy. Can you say Daddy?"

For a moment Asher was struck by the change on her face. He wished she'd smile at him like that.

For the first time he realized how fortunate he was that

she'd responded when he'd yelled for Sarah yesterday. He couldn't have handled these children by himself.

They stood by Charlotte, shaking their heads. Then Madison began talking nineteen to the dozen.

Charlotte listened as if she understood every word, nodding and smiling. Maybe she did.

But he didn't.

A father should be better able to cope. What was he going to do? Dealing on an international level in business was one thing. The thought of dealing with these toddlers scared him half to death.

Charlotte stayed in the reception area with the twins when Asher met with Addie's attorney, Thomas Randall.

The girls had warmed up to her, and she thought it best to have as few disruptions as possible. They already had experienced a lot of change. She'd try to make things easier for them.

Sitting on the sofa, she enticed them to sit beside her, one on each side.

"Let me tell you a story. It's about two big girls who just met their daddy."

Trying to explain the coming changes in a story, Charlotte told the tale in simple terms. She made flying sound like a grand adventure and moving to San Francisco as normal as brushing their teeth.

When Thomas Randall offered to read the will aloud, Asher asked if he could skim it himself. It took only a few minutes. The will was short and simple. The half interest Addie owned in the company was left in trust to her daughters, to be administered by her husband, the children's father.

Asher looked at the attorney when he finished.

"She was a young woman. Her death caught me by surprise," Asher said. He wondered how much the man knew about their marriage.

The attorney nodded.

"The children's nanny called us when Addie went into the hospital. I went to see your wife just before she died. She was very sick. I think she pushed herself too hard and had no reserves when the end came."

"The girls will miss her," Asher murmured.

"Not as much as you might suspect," Randall said. "Apparently there have been a series of nannies and housekeepers over the last couple of years. I don't believe the girls are strongly attached to anyone—even their mother. My receptionist reported they adjusted well to staying with her."

"I'll get them established in a stable environment. I have to return to San Francisco," Asher said.

"We expected that. I have all the paperwork right here. Anything else we can do, just ask."

"I'd like directions to the cemetery," Asher said as he began to read the legal papers that would wind up Addie's estate.

When Asher finished with the lawyer, he returned to the reception area where Charlotte sat on the sofa softly reading aloud, a twin snuggled on each side, their eyes on the pages of the book. For a moment they didn't see him.

He took the time to study the group, aware of a curious yearning.

That is what a family would look like. A mother devoted to her children, all of them waiting for the father.

He hadn't realized before that he had no clear vision of a family. He'd been raised by his grandfather, a gruff old man. There'd been few amenities or social graces in that all-male household, but at least he'd had his grandfather when his parents died.

He hadn't gone into foster care like Charlotte.

Nor would his children.

His goal for the last decade had been to establish his company, make it a success. He'd never given a thought to starting a family. Now he'd been presented with a ready-made one.

Was the next step to acquire another wife?

One of the twins looked up, the one who sucked her thumb. Kennedy?

"Man," she said.

Charlotte looked up.

"How'd it go?"

"Fine. I'm finished here. We can head for Addie's apartment. We'll need to pack the children's clothes and toys. I'll also have to get an idea of what's needed to close the place. Later I want to swing by the office and make sure things are settled there. Paul will be in charge. I want to review the current projects with him."

For a moment he thought her lips tightened, and he remembered her comment about having kids dumped on her. But it couldn't be helped. No matter her likes or dislikes, Charlotte looked like a natural with those twins. And he hadn't a clue how to begin.

It was only for a day. Then she'd be back in the office and

could stay away from children for the rest of her life if she so chose.

"As long as you realize you have to pull your own weight," she said, disengaging herself and rising.

"Come on, munchkins, time to go home. Kennedy, you come with me. Madison, you go with Daddy."

He almost didn't recognize the appellation. He was the *daddy* of these children.

Charlotte picked up Kennedy and propped her on her hip. She looked at Asher, her dark, solemn eyes behind her glasses. Was there a hint of a challenge in her gaze?

Asher reached down and picked up Madison. She was light as a feather. Holding her against his chest, he stared into her eyes. She patted his cheek and smiled. Something tugged in his heart.

She was precious. Small and alone and totally dependent upon him to care for her.

Panic nipped at his heels. Could he do it? What if he screwed up? He knew nothing about parenting.

Had thought to work up to it, if ever he'd decided to take the plunge. Read books while his wife was pregnant, learn as they went along. Not be an instant father with no warning and no time to prepare.

"Let's go, Daddy."

Amusement danced in Charlotte's eyes, but she kept the smile from her lips. No point in letting Asher know she found his uncertainty touching. He was a dynamo in the office. Now he looked as awkward as a teenager on a first date. She blinked and led the way from the reception area.

Why in the world had she thought about dating?

She was a temporary baby-sitter, that's all. He was dumping his children on her and taking off for the New York office, abdicating all responsibility for a day. Sometimes it didn't pay to open your mouth.

Adding the small bag for the twins to the others, he followed. Charlotte waited by the elevator, allowing Kennedy to press the buttons. Both were lit, but she didn't care. They'd just wait for a down elevator. Children liked to experiment and try things. She may be mad at their father for insisting she accompany him, but she'd never take that anger out on these children.

Addie Callahan's apartment came as a surprise. It was large, formally decorated in delicate Queen Anne furnishings and located in a prestigious neighborhood only two blocks from Central Park. When they entered, Asher placed Madison on the floor. She didn't move. Charlotte deposited Kennedy beside her. The two girls looked at the adults.

"Where's your room?" Charlotte asked.

Madison pointed down the hall.

Crossing into the living room, Asher dropped their bags on the floor beside an ornate credenza that took up most of the wall. Surveying the room, he wondered when Addie had decided to go for the elegant look. Their place in San Francisco had been comfortable with sturdy furniture and few knickknacks. Maybe this style fit with her idea of living in New York. He didn't like it much, but he was more interested in comfort at home.

"No, no," Kennedy said when Charlotte started to follow.

"What?"

"No, no." Kennedy shook her head, warily eyeing the

living room.

The phone rang.

Asher crossed to answer it, puzzled by Kennedy.

"Asher Callahan."

"Mr. Callahan, this is Annie Simmons. Mr. Randall called a little while ago and suggested I get in touch with you. I was the twins' nanny. The most recent one, I should say. I understand you'll be taking the children back to San Francisco with you, but if I can help in the meantime, please let me know. I don't start another job for a week."

"We plan to leave tomorrow." Asher glanced at Charlotte. "But if you could come by today, that would be great. You could help us pack their things, maybe suggest where I can dispose of what we don't take with us."

"Surely. I could stop by around one."

Asher checked his watch. It wasn't even noon. "That will be fine."

"I'll be there."

Charlotte and the twins had disappeared. He followed the sound of voices drifting down the hall and stopped at the door to their bedroom. It was large, with two cribs, a highboy dresser and more dolls and stuffed animals scattered around than most toy stores carried. Addie hadn't stinted on gifts for her daughters.

Kennedy stood near the wall, watching Charlotte and Madison, thumb firmly in her mouth. He wondered why one sucked her thumb and the other didn't. Of course in the short drive from the attorney's office, he'd noticed the difference in the personalities of the two.

Madison was outgoing and friendly. Curious and fearless.

Kennedy seemed to watch carefully, shy and quiet.

Interesting with identical twins. Or was that the norm? He had so much to learn.

"That was the girls' nanny. She'll stop by at one to help pack."

Charlotte nodded, took off her suit jacket and tossed it across the rails of one of the cribs.

The soft material of her blouse draped over her trim figure, Asher noticed. His eyes skimmed over her curves. Again he wondered what she'd look like in lacy, frilly dresses.

It was probably something he'd never see. She was an employee, here under protest to help him with his newly discovered daughters. Nothing else.

He shook his head. Who was he kidding? Only himself. Because he was the only one who knew about the attraction he felt around Charlotte Thompson. And it had better stay that way. A passing fancy. Once he caught up on sleep, got back into the routine of work, he'd move beyond any such awareness.

Or so he hoped.

"If you find the suitcases, I'll start packing," Charlotte said, opening a drawer in the high dresser. Might as well make the most of the situation. She could get started on packing, then sort favorite toys and books when the nanny arrived. She'd also make sure she found out as much as she could about the twins' habits, likes and dislikes. Poor babies needed all the help they could get, moving to an entirely new life-style.

She glanced at Asher, startled to find his gaze traveling over her. Heat flushed through. Swallowing hard, she shifted and turned her back. The unexpected tingling was not a sensation she'd felt before. She wasn't getting sick, was she?

No, it was the constant state of awareness she felt around Asher Callahan.

Clearing her throat, she thought longingly about her bag. She had jeans and a shirt in it. Maybe she should change before she did anything else.

"It may take me a while to find them," he said.

Asher went into the hallway and crossed to the second bedroom.

Find what? Oh, the suitcases for the children. Charlotte pressed her hands against her cheeks, feeling the heat. She was acting like an idiot. She was here to take care of his children. And she'd better remember that every single second.

She trailed after Asher and found him in what must have been his wife's bedroom. Addie's things still lay strewn about. The bed was unmade, as if she'd risen only that morning to head for the hospital.

A pang hit her.

Addie had been alone at the end. If his trip to Bangkok had been postponed, if the typhoon hadn't struck, Asher could have been with her.

"I'm sorry you didn't make it back in time," she said softly, watching the bleak look in his eyes.

"I didn't even know she was sick. She should have told me."

"Maybe she didn't think it was serious until too late. Maybe she didn't know how serious."

"I would have insisted the doctors try everything in their power to keep her alive."

"I'm sure they did all they could."

She longed to offer comfort, but was unsure what to say. Did he want to talk about it? Knowing human touch could help, she reached out and clasped his hand, squeezing a bit, just to let him know he wasn't alone.

"I don't know a thing about taking care of babies," he said, looking around the room.

But the tight grip of his hand let Charlotte know he didn't want to be alone.

"You'll learn what you need to know. And you can afford competent help to take care of a lot of the routine things."

A shriek of laughter came from the twins' room.

"I guess I'd better check on them," Charlotte said, squeezing his hand one last time before she slowly let go. For a moment he held on, then released her.

"I'll hunt up those suitcases."

Asher opened the closet door. Clothes filled the space. In the back, to the left, sat a matching set of expensive leather luggage. He drew the suitcases out, brushing against the clothes. He realized they still carried the faint scent of Addie's perfume.

He couldn't believe he wouldn't see her again, wouldn't go toe-to-toe with her over some business decision. Wouldn't hear her wild dreams, most of which had a basic, strong concept they usually implemented. Wouldn't argue about the rate of expansion and the cost-cutting measures he always demanded.

Shaking his head, dispelling memories, Asher returned to the children's room.

"The water is too cold to swim in. When you walk outside it will be windy some days, cool from the bay, but that's good for flying kites."

Charlotte chatted with the children as she stacked clothes on one of the cribs.

"What are you telling them?" Asher asked, looking for a place to put the suitcases.

"About their new home. I think they'll feel more comfortable knowing about the change," she said. "Just put them on the floor. There's no room anywhere else."

"Here, Madison, you put this in the suitcase."

Charlotte handed the toddler two folded shirts. Madison walked to the suitcase and dumped them in.

"Great technique, kid," Asher muttered.

Charlotte laughed.

"It doesn't matter. They want to help," she said as she handed a similar stack to Kennedy.

"Why not dump the drawers into the case if you're not going to neatly fold them?" he asked, watching the jumble of shirts steadily growing in the suitcase.

"When they nap, I'll fold everything. Right now this keeps them occupied and gives them the feeling they're helping, that they're participating in this move."

"Psychology, too?"

He raised an eyebrow, studying her.

"Practical, actually. You could help."

"You've got a system going. I think I'll check out Addie's things. See if I can find her personal papers and pack them. I'll have to get someone in to close up this place."

"Find some things of their mother's that the children can have when they're older," Charlotte suggested. "They won't remember her, poor babies, but it will be nice for them when they're grown to have something of their mother."

He heard the wistful note in her voice.

"Do you?" he asked softly.

Knowing he was treading on personal ground, he still had to know.

She shook her head.

"That's why I know they'll appreciate it. We had so little. I don't know what happened to our things. Social Services came for me, we packed my clothes, and I got to take one doll. That was all."

"That's tough."

He remembered his grandfather's complaining, when his parents died, about having to store furniture and boxes in that shed in the back. Most of it was still there—a link to parents he scarcely remembered.

"It was a long time ago." She smiled at him, her head tilted slightly.

"I'll find a few things for the girls. I could have everything shipped to the West Coast," Asher said, his heart skipping a beat at her smile.

"You're the boss. But they may not want this furniture. Just mementos."

Asher shrugged out of his suit jacket, slung it over one shoulder and headed for the living room. He tossed the jacket on the back of the sofa and looked around. The art on the walls was good quality.

The figurines and vases would make nice mementos. Had they held special meaning for Addie, or had she chosen them to complement the decor?

Odd he knew so little about a woman to whom he'd been

married for so long. He crossed the room, then paused by a small antique desk. The drawers contained Addie's papers—most recent bills, bank statements, address book and other items.

Asher sat down and began to go through everything.

By the time Annie Simmons arrived at one, Asher longed to escape the madhouse of the apartment and find some sort of order at the New York office of Callahan Associates. The girls ran back and forth between Charlotte and him.

They'd been hesitant at first to enter the living room, but he'd made it clear they could come to him when they wanted. Laughing, shrieking and running on their sturdy little legs, they displayed more energy than he'd seen in years.

Annie Simmons appeared to be in her mid-forties. The twins greeted her with happy smiles and hugged her, then began talking so fast he hadn't a clue what they were saying. Yet Annie and Charlotte both seemed to understand. Did women come with some sort of built-in translator?

"I'll miss these babies, that's for sure," Annie said after she'd listened to them for a few minutes. "They were so good. I'm sorry, Mr. Callahan, for the loss of your wife."

Asher nodded, feeling that awkwardness again. He wanted to stop by the cemetery on the way to the office. See where she was, if anything else was needed.

"We're hoping you can fill us in on the twins, what they like, what their schedule is. We'll be leaving tomorrow for San Francisco," Charlotte said, giving him an odd look.

"Be glad to tell you all I know. I watched them for five months. Children sure grow fast at this age. I swear they seem even taller than the last time I saw them."

"I'm going to have to get to the office. Charlotte, can you take over here?" Asher asked, anxious to leave.

She nodded. "Of course."

"Are you going to be the twins' new nanny?" Annie asked as Asher pulled the door closed behind him.

"No. I work in the San Francisco offices of Callahan Associates. I came to help Asher get the children home," Charlotte said quickly.

She didn't want anyone, even Annie Simmons, to think her new role in life was nanny to these children. This was a two-day assignment, that was all.

Though for a moment as she watched Madison run to the window to see if she could see the man leave, she wondered if she could stop by Asher's place once in a while to see them. They were so adorable and she was already growing fond of them.

Frowning, she led the way into the bedroom. She didn't want to form an attachment for these children. She had her future mapped out.

It was after five by the time Asher let himself into the apartment. Charlotte sat on one of the elegant wing chairs near the fireplace, a book opened on her lap. She had changed into her casual clothes—jeans and a soft yellow cotton top. She glanced up when he closed the door.

"Everything all right at the office?" she asked, marking her place in the book with a finger.

Rubbing the back of his neck, Asher nodded. He crossed into the living room and looked around.

"Things will settle down there soon. Paul Whitstone will make a good general manager. Where are the twins?" he asked, sinking down in the brocade-covered sofa.

"I put them down for a nap a little while ago. Annie says they nap every afternoon. After the activities of the day, I expect they'll sleep for a while yet. Though we should wake them up before too long, so they'll sleep tonight."

Loosening his tie, he lay his head against the sofa back. Charlotte watched him, considering how tired he must still be. Their flight hadn't been enough time to catch up on sleep. And he'd been going full blast all day.

"Tired?" she asked sympathetically.

The entire day must have been a strain, even without the lack of sleep.

"I'd like to go to sleep for a week."

"Sorry, we leave in the morning."

"Was Annie Simmons helpful in telling you about the twins?"

"I learned a lot. You should have stayed, however. What if I forget to tell you something or you have questions I didn't think to ask? I did get her phone number, so you can call her if you need to know more—like Madison throws tantrums if she doesn't get her way, and Kennedy runs and hides. Kennedy doesn't like eggs. Madison has a bigger vocabulary. And your wife didn't let the kids in most of the apartment for fear they'd ruin things. That explained their hesitation in entering the living room."

Asher heard the indignation in her tone. He wanted to smile. She might not like having kids dumped on her, but she stood up for them. Obviously she thought children should have the run of their home. Well, he did, too, as a matter of fact.

"Having been properly chastised, I'd like you to tell me more about these girls. What am I to do with them when I get them home?"

He leaned against the sofa cushions, listening to her voice. It was low and sweet.

"Hope that Sarah has found a nanny for you."

"Think I can't make it as a single father?" he asked, curious to hear her reaction.

He had his doubts. Did everyone else, as well?

"If today is anything to go by, you'll make a great father. You were quite patient with them, if a bit stiff. They'll need a lot of love, attention and guidelines."

"It would be easier if I had a wife."

33

Charlotte's gaze met his. For an instant she felt heat steal into her cheeks. She looked away and hoped he hadn't noticed. What would it be like to be married to Asher Callahan? To have him come home every night and discuss his day. To plan family outings for the weekend, to laugh together, love together.

She needed to get hold of her thoughts before she made a fool of herself. She rose and put the book on the shelf, keeping her back to him, hoping he was too tired to pay any attention to her. He was thinking aloud. It had nothing to do with her.

"I guess it would be easier, especially if you found a wife who wanted to stay home all day and baby-sit your children," she said coldly.

She'd hate to be chosen for marriage based on her child care ability.

"A woman who married me would become the children's mother. I don't think she'd see it as baby-sitting my children."

Charlotte shrugged and crossed the room.

"I'll check on the twins and then start dinner. Mrs. Callahan apparently didn't eat here much. There isn't a lot of choice."

"We can order something in. You don't have to cook."

Asher rose. He was a big man, Charlotte noticed, and seemed to fill the room just by his presence.

"I don't mind. I like cooking. We might as well use up some of the food, less to waste."

She hurried away, away from the thoughts that slipped into her mind and the vague yearnings that arose.

Asher watched her as she left the room. For a moment he toyed with imagining her reaction if he asked her to marry him. She'd been perfect with the twins. He'd feel better knowing someone who knew something about children was partly responsible for helping them grow up.

Of course Sarah would locate an experienced nanny. But a hired person could quit and leave. A mother would stay.

Slowly he turned and regarded the now empty chair. He could envision coming home from work each day and finding Charlotte surrounded by children, her hair loose, her glasses on the table and her wide eyes laughing at him as she told him about the children's antics.

He'd be able to forget business for a while and share the experiences of his children as they grew.

Frowning, Asher shook his head. Pipe dreams.

Charlotte Thompson had made it perfectly clear she was a dedicated businesswoman who, by her last comment, didn't see marriage with a man who had children as something to aspire to.

And after his marriage with Addie, he didn't think he wanted a business relationship again. It had worked. They'd accomplished what they'd set out to do, but next time he wanted more.

If there was a next time.

He grabbed his bag and headed for Addie's room. He'd take a quick shower and change into more casual clothes. He wondered if Madison and Kennedy would be even more energetic after a nap. He'd look forward to finding out—and getting to know his little girls better.

Entering the bedroom, Asher stopped as realization struck. There was only one bed, beside the two cribs, in the entire apartment. What were they to do tonight?

Granted, Addie's bed was king-size, but he had the distinct feeling that Charlotte wouldn't care if it covered half the apartment—she wouldn't share.

For a moment his imagination took over. Charlotte in his bed, her dark glossy hair spread across a pristine white pillow, her face alight with love.

Love? Hardly something to expect from a die hard businesswoman.

The sofa he'd vacated would never do for a bed—curving wooden arms, stiff brocade, as uncomfortable as museum furniture. It looked elegant but didn't lend itself to comfort.

He could get a hotel room for the night.

And have Charlotte berate him for deserting his children their first night together? Not likely.

He crossed the room, opened his suitcase, took out his jeans and a navy T-shirt and headed for the bathroom.

Maybe he could get her a hotel room.

No, he liked that idea even less. He needed her here in the apartment in case the girls woke during the night. He'd have to come up with something during dinner. Right now a hot shower was as far ahead as he could plan.

By the time he'd finished showering, Asher heard the chatter of little girls. Smiling as he pulled on his jeans, drew his T-shirt over his head, he realized he'd already come to expect some kind of noise around them. They'd sure change his place in San Francisco.

Change his entire life.

He'd have to look for a different apartment, something bigger. Maybe even a house with a yard. Would little girls want a dog?

The image of his grandfather's dog came to mind. How would old Ranger have dealt with the twins had he still been alive?

Come to that, how would his grandfather?

"Need any help?" he asked a couple of minutes later, entering the kitchen.

Anticipation had already built to see his daughters, to see Charlotte.

The twins turned and ran to him, holding up their arms. He leaned over and scooped both up.

"Hi, Madison, Kennedy. Did you have a good nap?"

Madison smiled and nodded vigorously.

"Lottie gib me carrot," she said, holding out the orange sliver.

"Me, too," Kennedy said, holding up a matching strip.

"Looks good. Maybe Lottie can gib me one," Asher said, crossing to stand beside her at the sink.

She smiled brightly, her glasses on the counter. For a moment Asher caught his breath. She looked beautiful. Her eyes danced in amusement. Color stained her cheeks, and her hair had slipped from the neat French braid. If he hadn't been holding his daughters, he would have slid a finger through the clasp and released it to let her hair fall around her shoulders.

"I can give you some carrots if you can do the hamburgers. I forgot how impatient hungry kids can be. If we both work at it, we can get the meal on the table faster."

Charlotte smiled at the three of them.

She hesitated, her smile fading as she took in his casual appearance. She'd never seen him in anything but a business suit before.

Somehow the casual navy T-shirt and snug-fitting jeans caused her mouth to grow dry.

He looked gorgeous, his hair a bit mussed and his arms full of tiny girls. His fatigue seemed to have vanished. He laughed at something Kennedy said. It made him look younger and far, far too attractive.

She needed to remember he was her boss.

"Hamburgers?" he asked, raising an eyebrow.

"There was a packet of frozen meat. I thawed it. I've got potatoes cooking in the microwave. I'll finish with this salad, and that will be that. We'll have to have the burgers without buns. There's no bread in the place."

Charlotte turned to the lettuce she was tearing and tried to ignore the clamoring of her senses to delve more into the exploration of this new image of Asher Callahan.

She had work to do, not fantasies to dream about.

"Okay. Want to help me cook hamburgers, girls?" Asher asked.

"No," Charlotte said, frowning.

Didn't the man have a clue what two-year-olds were

capable of? Or not, as the case may be.

"No?"

"Not around a hot stove. They can set the table."

He set them down and searched for the silverware drawer. The thought of the twins running with a fork in each hand sent shivers up his back.

"Maybe not. How about I entertain them and you do the burgers? I don't mind waiting."

"If you like."

"Lottie play wif me?" Kennedy asked, tugging on Charlotte's jeans.

"I'm busy now, honey, but Daddy will play."

Asher scooped them up and headed for their room, starting to grow used to being called Daddy by Charlotte. How soon before his daughters called him that?

By the time dinner was on the table, Asher had a new respect for parents everywhere. He had watched the girls for less than an hour and he was already exhausted—yet intrigued by these little creatures.

Their enthusiasm for everything knew no bounds. They shared easily, including him in their games and talked nonstop. He was catching on to their lingo.

His anger toward Addie simmered. How could she have denied him the chance to know his daughters? Had she *ever* planned to tell him? Had he overlooked some clue that would have informed him earlier of their existence?

Dinner proved an adventure. The girls didn't eat much, and half of what they tried to eat went on the floor, the table or their clothes. Taking a clue from Charlotte, however, Asher didn't worry about the mess or correct their behavior.

"They'll eat enough to grow, and the rest can be cleaned up. At least they feed themselves," Charlotte commented at one point, noticing Asher's uncertainty.

She'd been around children for years and knew they'd eat enough to satisfy them. No sense in making a fuss on their last night in their home. Tomorrow would be fraught with changes. Let them enjoy themselves tonight.

"I dread mealtime on the flight tomorrow," Asher said as Kennedy threw lettuce on the table, wrinkling her nose. Maybe it was something she didn't like.

"Discretion being the better part of valor, I suggest we carry only snacks that they can handle. Maybe some Cheerios, graham crackers, and juice."

"How many babies did you baby-sit?" he asked.

He never would have anticipated how even a sandwich for them might be a problem. What else was he in ignorance about?

"Lots. Mostly with my foster parents. They cared for a set of twins at one point. But they were older than these two—wild little boys."

She smiled. Somehow, looking back, it didn't seem quite so bad. Not that she wanted to get caught up in child care again. She liked her job and was good at it.

"So you have plenty of experience with all ages," he said, studying her thoughtfully.

"Yes."

She looked at him warily. His comment from earlier echoed in her mind. If he asked her to marry him to take care of his daughters, she'd throw something.

Asher smiled.

"Tell me more about your ideas for World vision. Did you factor into the equation their initial forays into global expansion?"

"Yes, I did, though they are a bit premature. However, I think we can point out the pitfalls and skirt around them for the time being. Once the firm is in a stronger financial position, I have an idea how to ease into what they really want. But it would be a mistake to rush the venture."

Without pause she reached out and caught Kennedy's glass just before she tipped milk on the table.

For the rest of the meal, they discussed business, interspersed with conversation with the two little girls.

Charlotte enjoyed herself and began to relax. It had been a long time since she'd done more than grab a bit to eat at the end of the day, more often than not eating out or having a quick sandwich at her desk while she worked late. She wanted to move ahead as quickly as possible and sometimes stayed hours after the rest of the staff had left.

Asher didn't voice his earlier thoughts about finding another wife. Charlotte chided herself for suspecting he'd have such a thought in mind for her.

In San Francisco, things would sort themselves out. She'd go back to her own life, and Asher would find someone to take care of his daughters.

"We'll do the dishes," he said when the twins clamored to get down at the end of the meal.

"I don't mind," Charlotte said.

Surprised he'd even think to offer, she felt another small kick in her heart. The man was thoughtful when he was not being dictatorial. She wouldn't have expected it. In fact, she was coming to better understand Asher with each passing minute. She'd never quite see him the same way in the office after this trip.

"You fixed dinner. We'll clean up. It was delicious, by the way. Thanks."

"It was hardly gourmet fare. Hamburgers, potatoes and salad."

"Still, it tasted good, and I appreciated not having to do it myself."

"There is that."

She smiled at the girls.

"Maybe I'll run a bath for them. When you're finished in here, we can pop them in and then get them ready for bed. Annie said they usually go to sleep around eight."

"Did you get all their things packed?"

"All the clothes, some of the toys. The rest will need to be sent. We'll be ready to leave early in the morning."

Which brought up the subject of where everyone would sleep tonight, she thought. Had Asher given any thought to the fact there was only one bed in the place?

She watched as he pushed back his chair, stacked the dishes and carried them to the sink.

Curious, she said nothing. She had an idea but would wait to see when he broached the subject. In the meantime, she'd make up the bed with fresh linens and run a tub for the twins.

"I'll push two of the chairs over so they can stand on them to be high enough to help," Charlotte said, suiting the words with action.

She lifted each child to a chair, admonishing them to be careful, then left him with his daughters. The new family needed time to bond. But she looked over her shoulder as she left, feeling just a little bit left out.

Help was definitely a euphemism, Asher thought a few minutes later. Madison loved splashing in the soapy water. Kennedy kept putting back the dishes and silverware as fast as Asher could place them in the drainer. At the rate they were going, each of them would be soaked, and it'd take until morning to finish the task.

Yet he didn't mind. Watching the joy in their eyes as they *helped* was more than worth the delay. No one had told him how enchanting young children could be. He wished he'd known about them since birth, had seen them take their first steps, heard their first words.

Then maybe he'd have a better chance of understanding them when they talked. He caught most of it, but sometimes they spoke to each other in what seemed to be their own private language. If he listened carefully, he almost caught on.

"Are you all going to stay here all night?" Charlotte asked from the doorway, amusement in her tone.

"Lottie, me help!" Kennedy said, turning and almost falling from the chair.

"Watch it, short stuff. Don't fall."

Asher caught her around the middle and set her on the floor.

"Bath time," Charlotte said, laughing softly as she took in the scene. "Though it looks as if you got a head start on me."

He surveyed the wet clothes the twins wore, his damp jeans.

"A new way to cut down on bath time. This is the soapy water phase, all you have to do is rinse them off," he said.

"Right. Come on, girls, you can play for ten minutes, then bedtime."

"Want story," Madison said as she clambered down from the chair, refusing help from her father.

"Me, too," Kennedy said, holding up her arms to Asher. He picked her up, hugged her briefly and set her on her feet. She ran after her sister.

Finishing the dishes in peace, Asher reflected on the day. A series of firsts from the start. He couldn't have managed without Charlotte. He'd have to make sure she knew that.

When they got to San Francisco, he'd ask her out to dinner as a kind of thank-you. Maybe they could try that place near the wharf that featured dancing. They could talk through dinner as they had tonight. Maybe do a little dancing.

He'd like to hold her in his arms and move to a slow beat. Feel that softly feminine body press against his as they swayed with the rhythm. Watch for the sparkle in her eyes. Surely she wouldn't wear a suit to dinner. Nor her glasses. Would she arrange her hair in a different style? Or let him unfasten the braid at some point during the evening?

Feeling decidedly un-daddy-like, Asher turned off the light and headed for the bathroom. The sound of splashing and childish laughter grew louder as he approached. Standing in the doorway, he watched as the twins did their best to evade Charlotte's attempts at washing. He liked her dogged determination mixed with laughter and teasing. She was good with them, patient and fun.

She was good with *him*, patient and fun. He found his eyes on her more than the children.

Kennedy spotted him and grinned. "Man," she said.

Madison looked up and grinned. He was still amazed at the identical faces that smiled at him.

"Daddy," Charlotte said, looking at him over her shoulder.

"Daddy, daddy, daddy," Madison chanted. Kennedy picked up the chorus.

"I'd offer to help, but you seem to have everything under control," he said.

"Don't you dare leave me alone," Charlotte protested. "Grab a towel and a kid. I'll take the other, and we'll have them ready for bed before they know what hit them."

It took longer than Asher expected, but when the little girls were dressed in matching Frozen nighties, their hair brushed out, smelling sweet and clean, his heart clutched. As he had all day, he tried to absorb as much about them as he could. He had a lot of catching up to do.

"Story," Madison said.

"Run and get a book, sweetie," Charlotte said, mopping the last of the water from the tile floor. She looked at Asher as he sank to the floor, leaning against the far wall.

Giggling softly, she tossed the towel into the empty tub, sat on the floor and leaned against the tub.

"Is this the same man who works through typhoons, letting nothing faze him? You looked wiped out."

"I feel it. Tell me this is because I'm still tired from the Bangkok trip."

Clamping her lower lip between white teeth to hold in her smile, she shook her head.

"That might have something to do with it, but it takes a lot of stamina to be a parent."

He rested his head against the wall, closing his eyes until they were open only a slit. She looked flushed from her exertions, warm and feminine. The glasses had stayed in the kitchen. Her hair was almost completely down.

He wasn't sure he could resist the temptation to finish letting it fall around her shoulders. When had he become obsessed with her hair?

"We have a shortage of beds," he said slowly.

She looked up and nodded. "But I have a solution. The bed in your wife's room is a king-size one—"

Asher held his breath. She was going to suggest they share? She didn't mind that they scarcely knew each other? It was a big bed, plenty of room for both of them to sleep without bothering the other.

If he played his cards right, he'd get to see that shiny dark hair spread on the pillow, see that sexy body in a frilly nightie—

"So I thought we could push it against one wall, and then the girls and I could sleep in it. I'd be on the outside so they wouldn't fall off."

He blinked and stared at her. She and the girls would share the bed? Where did that leave him?

"And I get the cribs?" he asked.

She laughed and shook her head. "Even if you could fit, you'd crash right through to the floor. But I did think you could put the two mattresses together end to end on the floor. That'd be long enough for you. Not the best solution, but it shouldn't be too uncomfortable. Unless you have another idea? I could go to a hotel, I guess."

He knew she'd never go for their sharing the bed.

"No, your plan is fine."

Asher rose and held out his hand to assist her up. Charlotte's hand was warm in his, smaller than he'd expected. She stood, her head coming to his chin. He could smell the sweet fragrance of her body, the soft floral scent and the warmth of her skin. It appeared as if she held her breath.

Slowly he reached out and flicked the clasp holding her braid.

"Your hair's coming down."

Before she could respond, he opened it, clenching the barrette with three fingers while his index finger loosened what remained of her braid.

Her hands tangled with his as she tried to tame her hair.

"I know it's a mess. I thought if you read the story, I could take a quick shower."

"I don't think it's a mess. It looks pretty."

Ignoring her hands, he continued to comb through the silky strands until they spread around her shoulders. The bright glare of the bathroom light picked up highlights.

Tilting her chin with his finger, he studied the effect. He felt a punch low in his stomach. She was beautiful. Her eyes wide and questioning as they stared into his, her cheeks flushed, her hair a glorious cloud around her face.

"Thank you for helping me with my daughters," Asher said softly.

Giving into impulse, he leaned over and kissed her.

For a second he thought she responded.

Then she pushed away, stumbling, almost falling into the tub. He caught her, waited until she gained her balance then stepped back.

"I'll see what story they want," Asher said.

He waited in case Charlotte had anything to say, but she merely nodded, her look one of startled surprise. He went to find the twins.

"Great," Charlotte mumbled as Asher headed down the short hall, "that had all the finesse of a hippopotamus."

Her boss gave her a brief kiss and she almost fell into a tub. She slapped her hands against her cheeks and she closed her eyes. How gauche could a woman be?

She was sadly out of practice. Not that she'd ever done a lot of dating, and the men she'd gone out with were nothing like Asher.

She had not expected a kiss—not from her boss.

Don't make so much of it, she admonished herself. She looked around, stunned. It had merely been a nice thank-you kiss for taking care of his twins. Slowly she let her fingers drift to her lips.

Somehow it seemed more than a mere thank-you. She remembered the firm warmth pressed against her, the scent that had filled her, the pounding of her heart. Swallowing hard, she glanced around again as if looking for something.

The bathroom was as tidy as they needed for tonight. Tomorrow the cleaning crew would arrive, and later someone from the New York office would take care of closing down Addie Callahan's last home.

Refusing to dwell on the kiss or her stupid reaction, Charlotte headed for the master bedroom. She'd take her shower and be ready for bed when the girls had had their story read.

Asher had pushed the large bed into a corner, urged the

girls into it and settled against a stack of pillows to read. The three of them looked up when she walked in.

"I'm getting my things for my shower," she said self-consciously.

Asher nodded and turned back to the story.

In only seconds Charlotte was behind a locked bathroom door, feeling as foolish as ever. What had she expected? That he would say something, try to smooth things over? She was the one who had overreacted.

Conscious of the man in the next room, she slipped out of her clothes and stood under the hot shower. For some reason she felt daring knowing he was so close. She'd never shared a place with a man, never spent the night with one. Never taken a shower with one.

He'd finished the second book when she returned to the bedroom.

"All done?" he asked.

Her hair was damp, hanging in waves down her back. She'd combed it, but it would have to dry overnight. After donning her sleep shirt, she realized she'd forgotten a robe. Somehow the shirt alone wasn't sufficient covering. She secured a thick bath towel around her, then felt brave enough to face him. Embarrassment seeped in as he looked at her with astonishment.

She was wearing a T-shirt, wrapped in a towel, her jeans and shoes clutched to her breast. No wonder—she probably presented a sight.

"Yes. Are you finished with the stories?"

She tried to act normal through the extraordinary circumstances.

"We just finished."

She shifted from one foot to the other, "Well, I guess I'll go to bed with the girls. I didn't get much sleep on the plane, and tomorrow will be another long day."

Asher glanced at his watch. It wasn't quite eight. He was so used to being so tired it seemed as if he'd been that way forever.

The dark smudges beneath her eyes attested to the fact she was also exhausted. He could understand why with the events of the last thirty-six hours.

He kissed Madison and Kennedy and scooted them over to make room for Charlotte, then rose, snatched one of the pillows and headed for the door.

Charlotte sidestepped as he drew closer.

"Will you wake me in the morning or do I need to find an alarm clock?"

"I'll get you up at six. Maybe we'll have a chance to get dressed before the angels wake up."

"Right, in your dreams."

She smiled shyly and edged toward the bed, dropping her jeans on one of the fancy chairs, setting the shoes beneath it. Asher left, and she took a deep breath. She dragged the towel from around her, then leaned over and began to dry her hair, chatting softly with the twins.

The door opened suddenly.

"Sheets! Where would I find bedding for my makeshift bed?"

Asher stopped, staring at her. The T-shirt she wore came to the top of her thighs, showing off her shapely, tanned legs, the curves of her body. She swallowed hard at the look in his eye, slowly dropping the towel until it hung in front of her.

"The closet in the hall has linens. I found them when I made up this bed."

She'd never had a man look at her with such blatant interest. Her heart skipped a beat and settled into a rapid rhythm.

"Right, see you in the morning."

Which may be forever in coming, Charlotte thought a half hour later. The girls had fallen right to sleep. Tired as she was, Charlotte couldn't sleep. Her thoughts spun, keeping her wide awake.

Her mind flitted between Asher's kiss and her stupid reaction, then to the echo of his words—maybe he needed a wife—and to her determination to build a career. These twins were adorable, very lovable. How had she gotten so tangled up in only a day?

"Charlotte?"

Gently Asher shook her shoulder. She rolled onto her back and her eyes flicked open, then closed. The room was dim. The early morning light didn't filter in through the drawn curtains. He had to see from the light in the hall. Charlotte slept on her side, the two twins cuddled up near each other. Even with three of them, the bed looked spacious.

"Hmm?"

He swallowed hard. A mass of wavy dark hair was spread out on the pillow. He could see the petite length of her beneath the light covers. The urge to slide in beside her was staggering.

"Charlotte, wake up."

Her eyes opened and she stared at him, a soft smile playing on her lips. Asher resisted the temptation to lean over and kiss her. Now was not the time nor place to indulge his yearning. He had a family to get home.

"What time is it?" she whispered, rising on one elbow and glancing at the sleeping girls, shaking her head to clear the last of the sleep.

"Just after six. I've called a cab to pick us up at seven-thirty. Can you be ready by then?"

"Sure. Did you start coffee?"

"I will."

But he made no effort to move, intrigued by this glimpse of her when she awoke. Was she one of those people who needed coffee before functioning? Or was she bright-eyed and eager to get the day started? Yesterday she'd been cranky. Would she be this morning?

"I'll be dressed in a jiffy," she said, sitting up and rubbing her eyes with her fingertips.

"Come to the kitchen when you're ready."

Reluctantly Asher turned and left the room. He'd start the coffee, see if there was anything perishable they needed to deal with before they left. He'd dressed in comfortable and—if last night was any indication—necessary jeans. His bag stood by the door, as did the two for his daughters. He'd left another for last minute items.

"That smells heavenly," Charlotte said when she entered the kitchen a few minutes later. She had decided as she dressed to treat the rest of the journey as lightly as she could. By the end of the day, she'd be home in her cozy apartment, the trip but a memory.

And if Asher happened to kiss her again—strictly to thank her for her help—she wouldn't fall apart. She'd be prepared.

"You ready to go?"

"Yes, I put my bag beside yours. As soon as we get the girls up and dressed, I can close theirs. Maybe we should plan to eat at the airport, what do you think?"

She talked fast, hoping to hide the fact she found him impressive in the early morning. His jeans were faded and old and fit with a comfortable snugness of long wear. His shirt delineated the firm muscles of his chest and shoulders. His skin looked smooth and warm along his jaw. And his eyes—

Charlotte looked away, knowing he'd seen her study him. So much for professional detachment.

"If they can wait that long. Coffee should be ready now."

She fetched two cups when the coffee maker stopped, and filled them. Handing one to Asher, she was careful to avoid touching him. Taking hers, she crossed a comfortable distance away and leaned against the counter, sipping the fragrant brew.

She cleared her throat and asked, "Did you sleep all right last night?"

He shook his head.

"Not a bit. The mattresses kept sliding apart. Every time I went to move, I fell through the connection and ended on the floor."

She smiled, taking a sip of coffee to hide it from him.

"Sorry about that. At least tonight you'll be home in your own bed. What are you doing about the twins when you get home? Did Sarah get cribs for them?"

Asher winced.

"I don't know. I never thought about it."

He glanced at the clock.

"Forget it. Don't you dare call her now. It's almost four o'clock in the morning at home. You can call her from the airport."

"See how important you are on this venture? Bedtime would have arrived before I thought about cribs."

"Glad I could help," she murmured.

In a way, she was. Still a bit miffed he'd made it an order, nevertheless she was glad she could help.

And he truly needed it.

"When we get home, I'd like to take you out to dinner one night," Asher said.

Charlotte looked up, her eyes wide.

"It's really not necessary."

"If it were necessary, I probably wouldn't want to do it. In this case, I do."

"Why?"

"As a thank-you for all this. Consider it a bonus for extraordinary work."

"When?"

"Friday?"

"What about the girls?"

"I didn't plan to include them."

"Who will you get to baby-sit?"

Asher had never given that a thought. Wouldn't the nanny Sarah hired take care of that? Yesterday afternoon, when he'd talked to Sarah, she hadn't found live-in help. It might take a little while, she'd said. He'd given her until this afternoon.

"I'll find someone," he said, suddenly feeling inadequate to the tasks ahead.

He knew so little about children and their needs. But he was more than willing to learn, and quickly.

"If you can find a sitter, I'll go," Charlotte said slowly, wondering if it were wise.

Once they returned home, they'd fall into boss and employee roles.

Dating co-workers was dangerous.

Not that dinner would be a date. He merely wanted to thank her for her help.

Asher was too relieved at her agreement to be annoyed by her lack of enthusiasm. Or was it caution? Now, wasn't that an interesting thought. His gaze roamed across the new T-shirt she wore, then to her snug jeans, then to her bright pink tennis shoes. She looked young and carefree and happy even with a dreaded baby-sitting trek on the plane still ahead.

How would she look on Friday night when he picked her up for dinner and dancing? He could hardly wait.

At the airport Asher checked in all the bags except the one shoulder bag Charlotte insisted they carry on board. The ticket agent had been most helpful in finding seats together in a bulkhead row with the aisle separating them—business class instead of first, but Asher didn't object. He wanted Charlotte to be close at hand more than he wanted the comfort of first class.

"What a lovely family you have," one of the passengers commented to Charlotte when she settled the twins in adjoining chairs in the waiting area.

"Thank you," Charlotte replied, throwing a teasing glance at Asher.

He met her gaze. What did she think of being tied with him and his girls? At least she hadn't made an announcement that she wasn't the mother and that they weren't a family.

She looked natural. Was there any way to convince her to stay with him, to become a mother to his daughters? The idea grew stronger every time it popped into his mind.

4

The plane ride went more smoothly than Charlotte anticipated and proved a lot more hectic than Asher expected. The twins were fascinated by all the different people, by the movie and the buttons on their seat arms. They disliked being confined in a small place, however. Once the beverage service was completed, Charlotte took turns walking each twin up and down the aisles until they grew tired. Thankfully, they napped for part of the journey.

Asher tried his best to entertain them when they awoke but was blatantly relieved when the final approach to San Francisco was announced. The flight had seemed longer than the one from Bangkok.

Charlotte smiled as she unfastened Kennedy's seat belt. Asher was fumbling with Madison's.

"Glad the trip is over?" she asked him.

"Glad we didn't have them on a trip to the Far East. I'm worn out."

"It's hard to stay in one place for long when you're only two," Charlotte murmured, patting Kennedy's hand and smiling at the child.

Charlotte thought they'd done very well. They were sweet little girls. Already she felt a growing attachment.

Shocked, she pulled away. She refused to let herself

become attached to Asher's daughters. She remembered every time a foster child had left after she'd started to care. How her heart had ached for months, missing them.

Even when she'd left to go to college, she'd missed Brandon and Sherry and little Tallie. She wondered what had happened to them. Were they happy? Had they also gone to college, found good jobs? A feeling of belonging?

Swallowing hard, she shifted her thoughts. She'd known Madison and Kennedy only a day, so she couldn't be growing attached. Besides, she could always ask Asher about them from time to time. Taking an interest in his children wasn't the same thing as becoming involved.

"I appreciate your help, Charlotte," Asher said as they gathered their belongings to exit from the plane once they reached the gate. "This was bad enough with an expert around. I don't think I could have managed alone and kept them so happy."

"You needed someone, that's for sure. But these are good children. You won't have any trouble with them," she said a bit wistfully.

They were beautiful children. Asher had a family now, people to whom he belonged and who belonged to him. She'd missed that growing up.

One day, when she was established, she'd start her own family.

"Easy for you to say. You'll be home in a little while. Right now, I'm not sure I can make it through until morning."

He lifted Madison into his arms. Slinging the diaper bag over his shoulder as if he'd been doing it for years, he stepped into the almost vacant aisle and waited for Charlotte and

Kennedy to precede him.

She flashed him a smile, taking in the charming picture of the large man holding such a tiny, feminine creature. For a moment she felt her heart melt.

That way lay danger.

Quickly, she walked up the aisle, refusing to let herself feel anything but a professional detachment. Once she helped Asher get the children home, her assignment would be finished.

With a feeling of déjà vu, Charlotte spotted a man holding a sign with Asher's name.

"Another limo?" she murmured as they approached the uniformed driver.

"It's cheaper than parking here. And a lot more convenient," Asher answered.

And a lot more luxurious, Charlotte thought a few minutes later when they were speeding toward San Francisco. The girls were buckled safely in their new car seats, and Charlotte sank back in the soft buttery leather.

"I could get used to this," she said appreciatively.

"Saves trouble finding a parking place at home, too," Asher said.

"Where do you live?"

Odd she hadn't asked before.

Of course, he was her boss. And she had no reason to know.

"Pacific Heights. In a nice old apartment with high ceilings and hardwood floors. Which—" he glanced speculatively at the twins "—I may have to carpet to keep the noise level down. When these two start running around, it'll sound like a herd of cattle."

"Is it large enough for live-in help?" she asked.

"Not really. I'll have to turn my office into a room for the nanny. Put the computer and files in my bedroom, I guess."

Charlotte nodded. There'd be a lot of changes in Asher Callahan's life. She studied the two little girls who gazed out the window in wonder. They were so adorable and sweet.

She'd dressed them in different colors, to aid in telling them apart. But she already recognized the differences. Their personalities were quite distinct. Did either resemble Asher? Glancing quickly at him, she wondered what his full personality was like. She knew he was patient, witness his dealings with the twins. And he rose to all challenges without complaint.

But was he truly happy to discover he had twin daughters? Would he be a loving, involved father? Or delegate their care to someone else? Would he get married right away just to obtain a mother for his girls?

For a moment, Charlotte had an overwhelming urge to insist he take special care of these children. To make sure he knew how important it was for children to feel loved and cherished. How devastated they'd feel if he did not.

But it wasn't her place.

Asher watched as the expressions chased around Charlotte's face. What was she thinking? He didn't know her well, but these last two days had been a crash course in Charlotte Thompson.

She was kind and loving to two unknown children. Snippy and irritated with him initially. Though he had to admit she'd never shown the girls a hint of that.

By dinner yesterday, she'd seemed resigned to the assignment and had put on a good face.

A pretty face, actually. He wished she'd take off those glasses again and loosen her hair. Looking away, he slowly drew in a deep breath. Thoughts like that led to the memory of their kiss. And remembering that put him in mind of other things he'd like to do with Charlotte.

Tomorrow they'd be back at work. Maybe then he could think of her as one of his marketing analysts, not someone he wanted to get to know better.

An uncomfortable thought came unbidden. What if he couldn't?

By the time the limousine reached his apartment building, Asher was growing decidedly nervous. Could he cope with these girls on his own?

He'd called Sarah earlier and, while she'd taken care of the furniture for the girls, she still hadn't located a live-in nanny.

It looked as if he'd be staying home for a couple of days until she found someone.

Charlotte carried Kennedy inside the spacious apartment. It was on the first floor, directly over the garages. At least there'd be no neighbors beneath them to complain about the twins running around. The hardwood floors gleamed in the afternoon sunshine. The windows were large, stretching almost to the high ceilings, and the curtains were light and airy.

She surveyed the furnishings in the huge living room. The word comfortable came to mind. Nothing like the fancy formal furnishing Addie had in her New York apartment. This furniture suited Asher.

And was much more suitable for two little girls.

The large stuffed sofa looked inviting. The easy chairs that flanked it had a well-worn look, as if many people had enjoyed sitting in them. There were books in the built-in bookcases, but few knickknacks to tempt a small child.

Slowly she placed Kennedy on her feet. The little girl had her thumb in her mouth. She leaned against Charlotte's leg as if afraid to break contact.

"Your room is down there," Asher said, setting Madison on the floor.

She tore down the hall. Kennedy watched her.

"Come on, pumpkin, we'll go see your new bedroom. Do you want to?" Charlotte said, reaching for her hand.

Curious to see more of his place, Charlotte was glad for the excuse.

The room had been hastily assembled. Two new cribs stood together near the wide window, an old chest of drawers pushed against one wall. There was a disassembled double bed leaning against the opposite wall and a comfortable rocking chair large enough for even Asher to enjoy.

"We'll have to get that bed out before it falls on one of them," Asher said as he followed her into the room.

He looked around then gazed at Charlotte.

"It doesn't look like their room in New York."

"No, but it won't take much to fix it up. A couple of mobiles and maybe some cutouts of Mickey Mouse or the Frozen pictures on the walls. If you got a toy box or shelves, they could put their toys away. It'll be fine, Asher. I think Sarah did a great job in only a day."

"This used to be Addie's room," he said slowly.

Charlotte's eyes widened. She knew they'd had a business

marriage but thought it had been the reason for getting married, not that they hadn't shared a bed. Obviously at one time they had, or the twins wouldn't be here. Not that it was any of her business.

"That'll be nice for them. You can tell them that when they're older."

"If we're still here. I thought I might look for a house or a bigger place. There's a park at the other end of the block but no backyard for them to play in."

"The place I grew up had a huge backyard. We had lots of fun playing there. Sometimes we'd camp out. We felt so brave."

She smiled in remembrance. Not everything had been bad in her childhood. She did have nice memories, and thinking about Madison and Kennedy brought some of them to mind.

"Well, I better be going," she said, turning.

"So soon?" Asher asked, all but blocking the door.

Charlotte struggled against a laugh. He sounded positively terrified.

"I believe my assignment has ended."

"Stay for supper, at least. We'll order pizza. Then I'll get a cab to take you home."

"All right. But only for pizza. Then I have to get home. Tomorrow's another workday, remember?"

"Thursday. And I suspect if you wanted to take the rest of the week off, the boss wouldn't mind," Asher said. "I'm that grateful for your help."

"I appreciate the thought, but I can't wait to get back to work. I want to get started on the next stage of the World vision project."

"Of course."

Asher's tone cooled considerably.

Charlotte looked up, startled at the change. He said nothing further, and she forgot about it when she began to unpack the girls' clothes.

By the time pizza arrived, the twins had explored every inch of the apartment. Charlotte had watched them while Asher moved the disassembled bed to a small room opposite the girls' bedroom. He'd set it up later so it would be ready when his hired nanny arrived.

The girls had never had pizza before, and Charlotte hoped the spicy sauce wouldn't upset their stomachs.

They each massacred a single slice and had a grand time. After a big glass of milk and slightly stale cookies Asher found in the cupboard, they were full and ready for a bath and bed.

Despite her intention to leave immediately after eating, Charlotte stayed to help get the twins ready for bed. Bath time was fun, with lots of splashing and giggling. Finally the two were settled in their new cribs.

"Thanks again, Charlotte," Asher said at the door of the apartment when she said goodbye, her bag and briefcase in hand.

The cab had arrived, and she had to hurry. But he was reluctant to let her leave.

"All in all, I guess I'm glad I could help," she said honestly. "And you only left them with me once," she teased.

He smiled. She'd had some moments of enjoyment with his daughters. And she was so good with them.

"So I'll see you tomorrow, maybe," she said brightly.

"Call me when you get home."

"Why?"

Asher shrugged, "Just to make sure you got there safely. I'll worry until I know you're home. Do you have my cell number?"

Charlotte stared at him. It had been years and years since anyone cared about her, cared if she were safely home at night. Warmth filled her heart. Smiling shyly, she shook her head, fishing her phone from her pocket.

Asher punched in his number and handed the phone back.

"Okay, I'll call as soon as I get there. Thanks for dinner," she said, replacing the phone in her pocket.

"If I get a sitter, we're still on for Friday night, right?" he asked, stalling.

"Right. Good night."

Asher reached out and drew her close, his mouth claiming hers in a brief kiss.

Charlotte's senses spun. Before she could react, however, he stood back and brushed his fingertips along her cheek.

"Good night."

So much for being prepared if Asher kissed her again, she thought wryly, walking down the single flight of stairs carefully lest she float into the stratosphere.

His kisses were amazing and her reactions even more so. But they didn't mean anything. She knew he was grateful for her help with the twins. That was all. A kiss of gratitude.

She tried to think rationally. But a part of her insisted on letting her imagination soar. His hot kisses were only the beginning. Soon Asher would fall madly in love with her, find her fascinating and irresistible. Ask her to marry him and share her life with him. He'd be so crazy about her that he'd do anything to keep her happy.

Maybe even make her a partner in Callahan Associates, just like Addie.

Abruptly her daydream ended. What was she thinking of? If he married her like Addie, it'd be a business marriage. And she didn't want to get married for years and years, not until she'd made a success of her career.

She suspected Asher planned to get married soon. He needed help with those twins, even with a live-in nanny. And hired help, no matter how competent, wasn't family.

Yet how could any woman be sure marriage to him wouldn't be solely so he could acquire a mother for his daughters?

She'd hate to be married as a convenience.

Not that any of her suppositions mattered. She had her plans laid out, and they didn't include watching children any time soon. Working had tapped into her creativity, her sense of order. She loved analyzing businesses, making recommendations for growth. For now, at least, her projects were her babies, and she wanted to see them attain fulfillment.

When she arrived home, Charlotte called the number Asher had given her.

"Home safe," she reported when he answered.

"Good."

"Are the girls asleep?"

"Yes, I haven't heard a peep from them. If Sarah can find someone tomorrow, I'll be at the office. If I don't make it in, feel free to call if you have any questions on the World vision project."

"Okay. Will do. Good night."

Businesslike and professional—the phone call was everything Charlotte wanted, so why did she feel so let down?

At work the next day, Charlotte plunged into the World vision project. She kept one eye on Asher's office. She realized by noon that he wasn't going to make an appearance. She wanted to know what Sarah had done about a nanny, but wasn't sure it was proper to inquire.

Twice she rose to ask and twice sat down. If Asher wanted her to know, he'd have Sarah tell her.

By mid-morning on Friday, Charlotte could stand it no longer. She headed for Sarah's desk.

"Good morning," Sarah said, looking up.

"Hi, Sarah. Asher in today?"

"No, I think he'll be back in on Monday. Need anything?"

"Just wondered how he was doing with the twins."

Sarah laughed softly.

"I think they're running him ragged. But he sounds curiously content with the situation. I found a woman who can move in over the weekend and start watching the girls on Monday, so things should settle into some kind of routine after that."

"Oh, good."

There was nothing else to say. Charlotte smiled and turned to leave. The phone rang.

"She's right here." Sarah held out the receiver. "It's Asher for you."

"Hello?"

"Hi, Charlotte? Look, I'm sorry about tonight, but I'm going to have to give you a rain check. Sarah's found a live-in nanny for the girls, but she won't be here until Sunday, and I don't have anyone to watch them. Can we postpone our date until next week?"

Date? She thought it was a thank-you dinner. She swallowed hard and nodded. Then felt like an idiot. He couldn't see her.

"Sure. That's fine. Do you need me to come over tonight to help out?"

Where had that come from? She'd sworn off watching other people's children. Yet she missed Madison and Kennedy. A quick visit couldn't hurt.

"No. We're managing. Actually the place is a total mess, and I'd just as soon not tarnish my image. But thanks for the offer. Sorry about tonight, I've been looking forward to it."

"Me, too."

She hadn't realized how much until he'd canceled.

"Put Sarah back on, please."

Charlotte handed the phone to the older woman and quickly returned to her desk. She could work as long as she wanted today on her current projects. She didn't need to leave early to get ready for a dinner date.

Somehow, the joy in the day vanished. For once the challenge of her projects didn't consume her.

By the time Charlotte opened the door to her empty apartment, it was after eight. She'd stopped by a Chinese place for dinner and wandered around Chinatown for a little while, window shopping. Feeling at a loose end, she planned to see if there was anything on television and maybe go to bed early.

As she changed into comfortable clothes, she remembered waiting for Asher to return to the apartment in New York. Even though she'd been alone while the girls napped, a simmering anticipation had filled her. It had been nice to hear of his day and tell him of hers.

Being married must be like that—to always have someone to share things with. Which she could do with her friends, she reminded herself before she could slip into a blue funk. But it wasn't the same thing.

When the phone rang, she wondered who could be calling her so late on a Friday night.

"Hello?"

"Charlotte, I need you."

Asher's voice came across the lines calm and dearly familiar.

"For what?"

Her heart sped up. Leaning against the wall, she smiled. It was good to hear his voice.

"Kennedy's sick, and I don't know what to do with her."

"What's wrong?"

She stood up, instantly worried.

"She's thrown up twice, complains her tummy hurts and won't stop crying. I've tried everything. Nothing seems to work. Any suggestions?"

"I'll be there in ten minutes."

"No, you don't need to come over, just tell me what I should do."

"I'll be there in ten minutes."

Charlotte hung up before he could protest and quickly phoned for a cab. She threw on a jacket and hurried outside impatiently. What could be wrong? Had the baby caught something from the crowd on the airplane?

She should have asked if Kennedy had a fever. Did Asher have a thermometer? What about fever-reducing medicines? She knew he didn't have any experience with children.

She should have made sure the basics were stocked.

Fifteen minutes later she ran up the steps to the first floor and hurried to Asher's door. She knocked impatiently.

Asher opened the door, a crying Kennedy in his arms. Madison hovered nearby, looking upset.

"Oh, baby, are you sick?"

Charlotte reached for the little girl, who lunged for her. Scooping her close, she hugged her, resting her cheek against the baby's forehead.

"No fever, just warm from crying, I think."

Relief flooded her. She'd imagined all sorts of things on the cab ride over.

"Man, I'm glad to see you, but I didn't mean to interrupt your evening."

"No problem, my date canceled," she said sassily. "Come on, babykins, tell Lottie what's wrong."

Kennedy snuggled closer and cried softly, her tears wetting Charlotte's cheek.

"Tummy hurts," she said.

Charlotte rubbed her back and smiled brightly at Madison.

"Hi, honey, how are you feeling?"

"Fine. Kenny sad."

"Yes, I see that. But she'll be fine soon."

Stepping into the kitchen, Charlotte looked at the chaos. There were plates and glasses stacked in the sink. Pans were on the stove and the trash was overflowing. She looked at Asher.

"Pretty bad, huh?" he said, looking at everything as if for the first time. "It's hard to get things done with two toddlers underfoot all day."

"And when they nap?"

"That's the only time I have for work. I do have a business to run, remember?" he said testily.

"Excuses, excuses," Charlotte teased.

Opening one cupboard after another, she searched for soup.

"What are you looking for?" Asher asked.

"Chicken noodle soup. You do have some, don't you?"

"Not that I know of. But canned goods are over here."

He opened a cupboard and began reading labels. Surprised, he lifted down a can. "I do have some."

"Probably courtesy of Sarah. Heat it up and we'll see if that makes this baby feel better."

Asher ran his fingertips over Kennedy's cheeks, brushing her hair from her flushed face.

"She'll be okay?"

"I think so. What did she have to eat today?"

Asher poured the soup in a saucepan, followed the directions on the can and turned on the burner.

"Just the same food she's been eating for two days. Except for the cotton candy."

"Cotton candy?"

"We went to Pier 39 today, to ride the merry-go-round. And I bought them some cotton candy."

Charlotte looked at Madison. "Does your tummy hurt,

honey?"

She shook her head.

"Do you think it was the candy?" Asher asked. "Madison didn't like it, said it was too sugary."

"Too sweet for her, huh? Too much sugar will make them hyper and could upset their stomachs."

Asher rubbed his eyes.

"I don't know how to be a father."

"Don't be silly, you're doing a great job. That was nice to spend the day at the pier, and I bet they loved the merry-go-round. But at this age, I wouldn't give them much beyond the bland foods they're used to. I was worried the other night about the pizza. They didn't eat too much, so it didn't upset their stomachs."

"I remember going to a fair once and getting cotton candy. It was so good."

"And you were probably older," Charlotte said, gently swaying back and forth.

Kennedy had stopped crying and snuggled close.

"I guess I was about nine."

"A tough little boy who could handle anything, even cotton candy."

Asher smiled slowly.

"I thought so in those days."

Charlotte's heart pounded. Heat slowly spread through her. Asher was devastating when he smiled. Her mind went blank. All she could do was feel the shimmering sensations that rushed through her as she stared at the man. She looked away quickly, afraid she'd melt into a puddle with Kennedy in her arms if she didn't gain some perspective. So he was handsome as sin. She had worked with handsome men.

She could handle this.

"Um, have you considered that if you don't tidy up a bit, your new nanny will take one look at this place and flee for her life?" Charlotte said, trying to get her emotions under control.

"Taken care of. Tomorrow my cleaning service is scheduled. I'm not crazy. The last thing I want to do is scare the woman away. Who would have thought it would be so tough to find a live-in nanny for two little girls? Sarah had a terrible time."

"I hope it works out. Is the soup warm yet?"

After Kennedy had a few sips of soup, she seemed improved. Madison stayed close to her sister. Only when Kennedy laughed at something Charlotte said did she relax.

"I want Mommy," Madison said to Asher, tugging on his sleeve.

He went completely still, gazing at his daughter.

"Your mommy's dead, honey. She's gone to live in heaven," Charlotte said gently as the silence stretched out.

"Should you tell them that?" Asher asked sharply. He looked angry. "They're just babies. When they asked earlier, I told them she had gone away."

"They are babies and probably will ask you a dozen times or more for their mommy. If you say she's gone away, it implies she'll be back. When she doesn't return, they'll question your credibility. They need the truth, no matter how difficult it is. And the truth is their mommy is dead and is never coming back for them. But they have their daddy, and he will take care of them. They need reassurance, Asher. Give them that, but don't lie to them."

"It seems so harsh."

"It is. But so is life sometimes. I think it's terrible they lost their mother so young. But they're lucky in that they have a father who will love them and take care of them."

"So they don't go to foster care or have to live with a cantankerous old grandfather," he murmured, caressing Madison's head.

"Who did that?"

Kennedy struggled to get down. Charlotte set her on her feet and watched as she and Madison rushed off to their room, sounding like that herd of cattle Asher had predicted.

"Me. My parents died when I was ten. I went to live with my grandfather. He wasn't pleased to have to raise me. He'd been a widower for years and had his life just the way he wanted. Raising a ten-year-old boy wasn't his idea of a peaceful retirement, but he was all I had. He had no choice."

"I'm sure he loved you."

Asher shrugged. "Maybe, but it wasn't a normal family life that most boys enjoy. I'd like for my girls to have a father *and* a mother."

Charlotte looked away. She'd be happy for him if he found some nice woman who would marry him and raise his children. The pang in her heart had nothing to do with disappointment or an unidentified yearning.

"So we're both orphans," she said as she rinsed the soup bowl.

The rest of the soup she'd put in the refrigerator in case they needed it later.

"Yes. Which is something I don't want for my children."

Asher leaned against the counter, watching as she stacked dishes in the sink, running water to let them soak.

"Better take care of yourself, then. You should live to be an old man. Is your grandfather still living?"

"Sure is. Eighty-three and going strong."

"What does he think about the girls?"

Asher shook his head.

"He doesn't know about them yet. I thought I'd drive up next weekend and introduce them. I imagine it'll come as quite a shock. It was for me. He lives in Sonora. Want to come with us?"

Yes, Charlotte wanted to shout. She'd love to spend a day with Asher and the twins next weekend. But caution warily took hold.

"I don't think so, but thank you for asking me."

"Well, I can't blame you. Baby-sitting on your day off probably doesn't hold much appeal."

"It isn't that. I'd love to spend the day with you and the girls. But it's a family outing. I'd be an outsider."

She'd had enough of that experience to last her a lifetime.

"No more than I feel around the twins. Come with us. Have you ever been to Sonora?"

She shook her head.

"You'll love it. It's an old gold mining town. Columbia is just a few minutes away. It's been restored to look just as it did during the gold rush. We could wander around and soak up a bit of history, education for the children, you know."

Charlotte laughed.

"Right, like a two-year-old is going to absorb a lot of California history in a weekend."

"You never know what they'll pick up. We'll have lunch and visit with Grandpa. He'll probably nap when the girls do. But I'd bet he'll watch them in the evening, and we could have that dinner together—just the two of us."

"That would mean going for the weekend," she said slowly.

The picture he painted tantalized. She'd love to see some of the gold rush country. And spend time with Asher.

Childish laughter sounded in the distance, but Charlotte scarcely noticed. She was mesmerized by the intensity of Asher's dark eyes, by the pull of attraction that threatened to spring out of control. And by the enticing image of a weekend in the gold country.

"Is there a problem? Do you have something else planned?"

His voice was low and deep. Its attraction pulled, as did the look in his eyes. Swallowing, Charlotte tried to discover a reason she should say no, but found none. It couldn't hurt to spend a couple of days with the Callahans. And she'd get to see a part of the state she had yet to visited.

It was always good to expand one's knowledge about history.

"I guess there's not a problem. What time do you want to leave?" she asked.

He smiled again. Maybe she should warn him about doing that. If he wanted her to keep any sense at all, he had to stop.

But in the meantime, she'd enjoy the shivers that danced up her back.

"We'll leave early. It takes about four hours."

"Add another half hour at least, to allow for extra stops."

"What extra stops?"

"Obviously you've never traveled with kids. Trust me on this, you'll have to stop several times."

"You're the expert. We'll leave at seven-thirty."

Charlotte looked around the kitchen.

"Want help in here before I go?"

Asher stepped closer.

"No. I told you the cleaning service is coming in the morning. They can handle it. Do you have to leave? Stay until after the girls are in bed. We didn't get dinner, but maybe we could spend a little time together. Unless you had other plans?"

"No, no other plans. And it's after nine. They should be in bed."

Charlotte considered the fire she was playing with. It was dangerous, but she had no inclination to leave. She liked being with Asher. And he could teach her so much about business. Maybe they could work a trade—child-care suggestions in exchange for coaching in business situations.

Putting the girls to bed was fun. Once they had their nighties on, all of them snuggled together on Asher's sofa to read Dr. Seuss's *Green Eggs and Ham*. Charlotte had read that book so many times she could recite sections without looking. Madison and Kennedy thought it wonderful. And she suspected Asher did, as well, from his look of amazement.

"You feel all better, Kennedy?" she asked as she tucked the toddler in her crib.

"Kenny better. Where's Mommy?"

"Mommy is in heaven. She misses you like you miss her. But your daddy's here, and he'll take care of you forever and ever."

Kissing the little girl on her cheek, Charlotte smelled the baby fresh skin with its hint of talc. Why did babies smell so good? They were precious enough without that added bonus.

She went to kiss Madison while Asher bid Kennedy goodnight. Then the two adults crept into the living room.

"They should be asleep in five minutes, if they stick to their routine," Asher said, stretching. He rolled his shoulders and looked at Charlotte.

"Thanks for staying, Lottie."

She raised her eyebrows at the diminutive.

"Do you mind?" he asked.

"Calling me Lottie?"

"The girls do it. They talk about you all the time. I guess I think of you now more as Lottie than Charlotte."

"It's fine."

Feeling flustered, Charlotte moved to look out the large window. The view of the apartment building across the street was not particularly inspiring, but it did look nice with lights shining from the windows.

"If you open the window and look to your right, you can catch a glimpse of the bay," he said, moving to stand right behind her. As he reached to unfasten the window, Asher pinned her between his hard body and the windowsill.

Charlotte resisted temptation to press herself against him. She watched as his long fingers unlatched the window and raised it. She stuck her head out and looked. In the distance she caught a glimpse of the sparkling lights on the Bay Bridge, their reflection dancing on the dark water.

"So this is a bay view apartment," she murmured as she

ducked her head inside and stood up. She was trapped by Asher.

"So they said when we rented. Does your apartment have such a view?"

His voice was low, seductive. He didn't move, just waited patiently as if to see what she would do.

Heart pounding, Charlotte vainly attempted to ignore the excitement that exploded. He was inches away. She felt his warmth encircle her as his arms encircled her.

Mesmerized, she froze as his head slowly descended. Giving herself up to the pleasure she knew he promised, she closed her eyes and met his kiss.

Had she waited all her life for such a kiss? His lips were warm and firm and oh-so-sexy as they moved against hers. He drew her to his hard length, and she reveled in the sensations that raged. Her arms encircled his shoulders, her fingertips tracing the edge of his hair, plunging in to feel the thickness, the heat. To hold on when her knees grew weak and her legs threatened to give way.

Breathing became difficult, but she didn't care. Her heart pounded so hard she could feel it against her chest. She never wanted to move. It was heaven on earth to be kissed by Asher Callahan.

"Daddy!"

A splash of ice water could not have ended the kiss any faster.

Asher turned and hurried into the bedroom. Charlotte took a deep breath and leaned against the windowsill. The coolness of the night began to counter the heat of his kiss, and in a moment she regained a modicum of common sense. Once she felt under control, she closed the window. Straightening her glasses, she wondered if she should leave.

An involvement with Asher was foolish. He'd want more from her than she could give. He'd almost admitted he planned to acquire a mother for his daughters. Was he pretending something else to lure her into accepting an offer?

It was hard to be practical sometimes. How could a few kisses hurt? He knew she was intent on building a career. As long as she made herself clear, he'd understand. She suspected he would soon make a concerted effort to find a wife. But in the meantime, they could spend a little time together.

And she enjoyed being with Madison and Kennedy. Smiling, she remembered their funny rendition of the merry-go-round they explained to her. They had been so enchanted with it.

"Sorry about that. Madison wanted a glass of water."

Asher returned to the living room but stayed near the door.

"A classic stalling technique. Effective, too. Now she'll be up sometime in the night needing the bathroom."

He smiled and nodded. "Same as last night. But I don't mind."

Taking a deep breath, Charlotte pushed away from the window and went to sit on the sofa, refusing to let her disappointment show. There was no reason for him to resume kissing her. Though from the way he looked at her mouth, she knew he was considering it.

5

Asher sat on the sofa beside her, careful to leave an appropriate distance between them. Stretching his long legs out in front of him, he leaned his head against the cushions.

"I'm tired. Those two can run a person ragged."

Charlotte was touched by the vulnerability she spotted. At the office he seemed so competent, so distant. He didn't tolerate incompetence or sloppy work.

She was fascinated by this private glimpse of him at home. The evidence of how different his life was now showed in the toys strewn about and the dirty dishes in the kitchen. Yet he hadn't showed any impatience with his children.

And he'd made their day memorable by taking them to a merry-go-round.

Her heart melted a little at the attempts this man was making to cope with instant fatherhood.

"They have so much energy. Yet think how exciting everything is for them at that age. So much to discover," she said.

"And so much danger. I thought I'd lost Kennedy at one point today at the pier. For a few awful moments I feared she'd fallen into the water or that someone had kidnapped her. And taking two little girls to the rest room isn't as easy as you might think."

Charlotte laughed softly.

"Asher, I really like your daughters, but do you think we could not talk about them for a while?"

He turned his head slightly to look at her.

"Anti-children. I almost forgot."

"Sort of, I guess."

"Too bad. You're so good with them."

"People can be good at things they don't like."

"Deliver me from being a doting father who bores everyone with tales of his brilliant children," he murmured.

"It's not that, Asher. They're adorable. I really like them. But—"

"But you have a career and no time for kids."

"I guess."

Put that way, it sounded cold.

Charlotte frowned. It wasn't that she didn't want children at some point, just not now.

"If the twins are off limits, so is business," Asher countered.

Charlotte stared at him. She'd wanted to pick his brain, explore different avenues of the projects she was working on. Obviously he'd seen through her.

"Fine. You pick a topic."

"I pick you," Asher said, smiling wickedly.

"Me? There's nothing remotely interesting about me. Besides, you already know everything about me."

"What I know is that you were born in LA and now live here. Somewhere along the way you went to college. As I recall from the interview, you had a list of impressive achievements."

Basking in the glow of his unexpected compliment, Charlotte relaxed.

"I love chocolate ice cream and like to read more than watch television. I like nice clothes but am secretly more comfortable in jeans. Is that what you want to know?"

"It's a start. What kind of books do you like to read? I like mysteries, myself."

Time seemed to fly as the conversation shifted from books they liked to movies they had and had not seen. Asher spoke of the travel he'd done for the company, and Charlotte confessed her longing to visit exotic locales.

When Asher rose to check on the girls, Charlotte almost went with him. She knew she was being foolish to keep a distance from the twins. Every child benefited from love, no matter who gave it.

But she was afraid she'd get caught up in feeling needed and wanted to the detriment of her professional goals. It would be so easy for a woman who had never had a family to yearn for one. To forget for a moment her true goals and give in to the fantasy of being part of a loving family.

"Asleep?" she asked when he returned.

"Fast asleep. Thanks for your help with Kennedy. I didn't know what to do."

"You need to get a pediatrician. If she had been really sick, you would have had to go to the hospital and take whoever was on call."

"There's more to this parenting that I expected."

"And you've only just started," she said with a smile. "But you're doing great, Asher. Don't worry about it."

"I like feeling in control, and this evening I felt anything but. I think women are better at this than men. If I had a wife, she'd have known what to do."

Charlotte's heart fell.

"Being a woman doesn't automatically mean she comes with an instruction booklet on how to raise children. Many men successfully raise children. And there are a lot of career women who haven't a clue."

"Like Sarah. I called her before you and she didn't have a single idea except to call you."

Feeling a bit deflated at being second choice, Charlotte checked her watch.

"It's late. I should be going."

"I'll call a cab. Thanks for staying. Talking with toddlers for two days, I was starved for adult conversation."

Charlotte didn't think he looked starved for anything. She watched him punch in the taxi number. His snug jeans looked worn and comfortable. He'd mentioned he also liked casual clothes more than business attire.

Somehow he looked even sexier in his faded jeans than his Armani suits. The way his broad shoulders filled his shirt sparked her memory of how those shoulders felt beneath her questing fingertips.

She rose abruptly and wandered around the room, trying to escape her thoughts.

Would he kiss her again before she left?

Thinking about the possibility had her tingling.

"It'll be here in just a few minutes. I didn't realize how late it was. Time went fast."

Asher went to the window to watch for the cab.

"I had fun. I'm glad Kennedy's okay. Upset tummies usually have a fast recovery. If she'd been truly ill, I think Madison would have been feeling bad, too."

"I wish I could walk you downstairs or even see you home," Asher said, leaning against the wall beside the window.

He could see the street and watch her at the same time.

"I'll be fine."

"Call me when you get there."

That unexpected warmth again. She nodded.

"He's here."

Asher crossed to her and rested his hands on her shoulders.

"I'll see you at the office next week. Then on Saturday we'll go to Sonora. Wear jeans, but bring a dress for dinner."

"Okay."

She was having trouble breathing. Every breath filled her with his special scent, a hint of musk and something else that was uniquely Asher.

He stared into her eyes for a long moment. Charlotte held her breath, too uncertain to initiate a kiss yet yearning for one with all her heart. Surely he'd kiss her good-night. He'd kissed her earlier.

Another thank-you kiss.

A goodbye kiss would be different, wouldn't it?

"You'd better go," Asher said, squeezing her shoulders gently and releasing her.

"Bye."

She almost ran from the apartment. Had he suspected how much she wanted a kiss? She'd die of embarrassment if he had. But she played it cool. Settling in the back of the cab, she glanced up at the lighted windows. He waved. She waved back and wished more than ever that he'd kissed her again.

On Monday Charlotte beat Asher to work by a solid ten minutes. At her desk when he arrived, she let herself enjoy looking at him, her gaze following him when he strode off the elevator. Already focused on the business at hand, he never glanced her way.

Disappointed, she plunged into work, trying to convince herself it was what she wanted. This was business. No time for personal agendas. But a quick wave or smile wouldn't have hurt.

Still, she had the weekend to look forward to. Two days with the twins and their sexy daddy.

Sexy? She stared blankly at the paper but saw only Asher's dark hair, tousled. Saw his laughter when listening to Madison explain something, the intensity of his eyes just before she closed hers when he kissed her.

He was sexy—and off-limits. She had work to do. Heat stole into her cheeks, and she ruthlessly brushed aside her thoughts before they distracted her so she couldn't do her job.

She didn't see Asher the rest of the day. Curious as to how he liked the new nanny, she wished he'd at least stopped by her desk long enough to tell her about the woman.

The first thing on the day's agenda on Tuesday was the regular staff meeting for project managers. Charlotte took her usual seat at the far end of the table from Asher. He joined the gathering at precisely nine and instantly began requesting information to bring him up to speed on various projects.

When it was Charlotte's turn, she spoke clearly and concisely. His gaze never wavered from her face while she spoke, but there was nothing in his expression to suggest he'd kissed her several times and had invited her to spend the weekend with him and his family in four days.

His treatment was professional and courteous, as with all his staff. The meeting went on a long time, since Asher had been away from the office for over a month.

Charlotte took a late lunch when the meeting ended.

The wind was brisk in the city streets, refreshing and invigorating. Charlotte loved to wander around at lunchtime when the weather permitted. San Francisco continued to charm her. Taking her deli sandwich to Union Square, she found a sheltered bench and basked in the sunshine, the cool air whipping strands from her neat French braid.

She and her team were making good strides on the World vision project. She was in the last stages of two other projects and already thinking ahead to a new idea for an old client. Her career seemed firmly established. In time she might even think of opening her own firm or going into partnership with someone.

Asher sprang to mind.

Giving in to the inevitable, she let herself dream about becoming a partner with him. They could travel together. Expand the company until theirs was one of the premier firms in international consulting in the Pacific Rim. She liked analyzing business directions and devising plans.

How much more exciting would her job be as her expertise grew?

But her thoughts didn't stay on business opportunities.

They veered to Asher himself. Remembering when she'd watched him pick up a daughter and toss her in the air, taking delight in her joy. Remembering him tired and quiet on the sofa, discussing music that appealed to him in different moods. She remembered Asher vulnerable and uncertain about how to provide the best for his daughters.

The strongest memories were of Asher's kisses.

Charlotte shook her head abruptly. Crushing the paper that had wrapped her sandwich, she rose, ready to return to work. She'd wasted enough time in foolish daydreams.

When Charlotte arrived at work on Thursday, the place was humming. A major client was expected at ten. The presentation the senior management team had prepared, if sold, would bring in a huge influx of cash and push the reputation of Callahan Associates even higher.

While Charlotte hadn't been involved in the project, she felt the same air of anticipation the team members did. She wanted the presentation to go well. She took pride in her firm.

Shortly before ten, Sarah hurried to her desk, a worried frown on her face.

"Charlotte, can I speak to you privately?" Sarah asked, her gaze darting nervously at the nearby desks.

"Of course."

Charlotte rose and followed Sarah to Asher's office. Sarah closed the door behind them.

"We've got an emergency on our hands. The nanny I hired for Asher quit without notice this morning. I'm trying to get someone, but so far no luck—at least I can't get anyone to watch the girls immediately. And the presentation to Moran Group is due to begin in less than a half hour. Asher has to be here. I don't know what else to do. Would you go watch the girls?"

"Me?" Charlotte asked. Not again.

"I know it isn't your regular job, but this is an emergency. If I could tell Asher you're coming, it'd go a long way to relieving his mind. The girls know you, and you know how to handle them. I wouldn't ask if it weren't so important. Please?"

"Did Asher ask you to get me?" Charlotte asked, growing cold at the thought of her hard work being ignored so she could function as a convenient nanny.

"No. He thinks I'm still trying the different agencies. If you refuse, I might have to go myself, and I don't know anything about children. Plus I was to provide the coffee for the group and be ready to make photocopies if needed and take minutes."

Sarah wrung her hands, obviously upset.

"Of all the days for this to happen. Why the woman couldn't have waited the week out I don't know. Please, Charlotte, it's just for today. Tomorrow Asher can stay home with them until I can find another nanny. But not today. This meeting's too important."

"Let me think," Charlotte said, trying to remember all she'd planned to do that day.

"I was analyzing some of the Hong Kong information from World vision."

"Use Asher's computer at home—it's linked up to the one here. He uses it all the time. If you can work from there, all the better. How about it?"

Sarah looked at the clock. It was almost nine forty-five.

"Okay. I'll get my papers and leave immediately."

"Let me call Asher first."

Sarah punched in his phone number.

"Asher? No, I didn't find anyone yet, but Charlotte said she'd watch them. ...Okay, I'll tell her."

Sarah hung up and grinned.

"Thank you, Charlotte. Asher said you saved his life and that of the firm and he'll be forever in your debt. He's bringing the girls here. You can meet them downstairs. There's no time for him to wait for you to get there before leaving for the office. Not if he wants to be on time for the meeting."

"That'll give me a chance to get my stuff together."

Feeling torn, Charlotte returned to her desk. She was glad to help—she wanted to be viewed as a team player. But somehow she didn't see a role as chief baby-sitter doing much to advance her career.

Still, it was nice to have the owner of the firm feel in her debt.

Charlotte waited in the building's lobby. She had all the materials she needed to finish her analysis of the Hong Kong market in her briefcase. As long as she could use Asher's home computer, she'd be fine.

Of course she'd only be able to work when the girls napped, but at least she'd have a few hours. And maybe she could bribe them with something on the TV to keep them occupied.

Asher hustled through the tall glass doors, a child's hand in each of his. The little girls had to run to keep up with his long stride. He looked harried and rushed—and downright wonderful.

Charlotte felt her heart rate increase.

"Lottie, you're a wonder."

He leaned over and kissed her lightly. Stooping to eye level with the twins, he looked at them.

"You two be good for Lottie. Mind her and don't get into trouble. Okay?"

Both girls nodded solemnly.

"'Kay, Daddy," Madison said.

"Me, too," Kennedy said, then gave Charlotte a sunny smile.

He rose and handed them over to Charlotte. He then handed her the key to the apartment.

"I don't know how late I'll be. I had planned to take the clients to dinner, but if I can get out of it, I will."

"Don't worry about it, Asher. Do what you need to get the contract. I'm going to use your computer and can keep working tonight if you're late. I'd probably get more done once they're in bed. Good luck."

His eyes gazed into hers for a long moment.

"Thanks, Lottie, I owe you."

He brushed his lips against hers again and strode to the elevator.

She watched him wistfully, wishing she was going back to the office with him, wishing she were participating in the presentation.

"Lottie play wif me?" Madison asked, smiling.

"Yes, Lottie will play with both of you. But first we have to go to my house so I can change my clothes. Then we'll go to the park, have lunch and take a long nap. Won't that be fun?"

Thankful for the limo at her command, she and the girls were back at their place in no time.

When the girls napped, Charlotte took her briefcase and headed for the door to Asher's bedroom. Conscious of the king-size bed that dominated the room, she gazed around, looking for the computer. It was set up on a small table against the opposite wall. She stepped inside and took a breath.

The room smelled like Asher. Instantly her senses came alive. Gazing at the bed, she saw the left pillow still bore the indentation from his head. So he slept on that side. Did he every night? He was a big man, probably liked the space the large bed provided.

His closet door was slightly ajar, displaying a row of suits and shirts. She closed it lest she found herself distracted. It was bad enough to have his bed just a few feet behind her.

There was a bathroom adjacent to the bedroom. Spotting his shaving paraphernalia, she walked to the door and studied the room. He hung up his towels and didn't leave his clothes lying around, she observed. But the cans and jars sitting on the counter looked foreign to her eyes.

She'd never shared a bathroom with a man. What would that be like? Would he mind if she perched on the edge of the tub and watched him shave? Did he do it right after a shower or did he partially dress first?

Stepping back, Charlotte shook her head. She had a few precious hours to work while the girls slept. There was no time to daydream the minutes away.

It was after ten when Charlotte heard the key in the lock. Asher came into the living room and stopped when he saw her. Slowly he smiled.

"How did it go?" she asked, rising from the sofa.

She'd finished her analyses a few moments ago and was glad to be in the living room rather than in his bedroom. Her glasses were on the table, and she'd let down her braid, running her fingers through her hair while she worked on the complex numbers. She should have brushed her hair. Too late now.

"They signed at four this afternoon. We went to dinner at the Blue Rose. I just dropped them at their hotel."

"Congratulations. I knew you could do it. I've heard about the plan from Bob Farrel. It sounded ambitious but made perfect sense. With a little bit of luck, it should implement flawlessly."

She grinned as happily as if it had been her project.

"I'm counting on it."

He shrugged out of his jacket and tossed it on the back of the sofa.

"How were the girls?"

"Angels. They're very well behaved."

He rubbed his eyes with his fingertips, then looked at her, slowly shaking his head.

"Not with Andrea Good. She was the nanny Sarah hired."

"What happened?"

Charlotte wished she felt comfortable enough to touch him, to offer a bit of comfort to ease his frustration.

"She'd been watching a young teenage girl for a family in Hillsdale who just got transferred to Belgium. Not wanting to move to Europe, she gave notice. But I suspect from what she said that the girl was a paragon of perfection. Madison and Kennedy seemed to be much more rambunctious. Into everything, according to Andrea."

"But why give notice in the middle of the week? Didn't she realize how that could impact on you?"

"I don't think she cared. This morning while she was dressing, the girls got into her makeup in the bathroom and made a huge mess—of themselves. And spilled or dumped all her bottles and creams. They mixed powder in with toothpaste for a nice effect."

Charlotte burst into laughter.

"I bet they thought they were beautiful. Now I know what they meant when they said they were pretty this morning. So Andrea didn't appreciate that, huh?"

"I'm glad she's gone. She was too old for them, I think. Always wanted them to sit quietly. I have yet to see them sit quietly."

"Except when being read to," Charlotte said, a smile still lighting her face.

Asher stared at her, his attention drawn from his daughters to the woman before him. She continued to fascinate him. He'd tried to keep his interest to a professional level. Even managed on Tuesday to treat her like every other employee.

But seeing that dark hair swirling around her shoulders made his fingers itch to touch it. Her eyes sparkled at him, no longer hidden behind the guardian glasses. She had looked as happy with the success of the Moran Group proposal as he felt.

He wished she'd been at the meeting, had attended the celebration dinner. It would have been nice to have someone who'd be pleased for his success beyond what it added to the company's bottom line.

To be genuinely happy for him.

"I appreciate your filling the gap so quickly. This afternoon Sarah found a young woman who will able to watch them during the day. She'll continue to look for live-in help. It seems to be a bigger problem than I thought to hire someone."

"Time for you to get that wife you keep talking about," Charlotte said lightly.

Asher nodded, watching as she gathered her things. His one foray into marriage hadn't been typical. For all the years he and Addie had been married, they had spent remarkably little time together. And when they had, more often than not their conversation had focused solely on business.

He felt he knew more about Charlotte after a week than he'd known about Addie in all the years they'd been together.

Charlotte would never have hidden the fact that he'd become a father.

But she was consumed by business, just like Addie.

Asher punched in the phone number of the taxi service.

"I ought to set this number in speed dial," he said.

He saw her hesitate, then raise her head to look at him, wary caution in her gaze.

"I don't plan to make this a habit."

"I sure hope we don't. You're too talented to spend all your time with children."

Grimly he watched her bloom beneath his casually spoken words. She was great with his children. It wasn't only the experience she'd garnered while growing up, it was her innate warmth and genuine interest. She was talented in business savvy, but she was gifted in dealing with children.

Asher watched from the window when Charlotte got into the cab. This made the third time. Wasn't there some saying about it being a lucky charm? He was getting used to this. Though he wished he could take her home, see her apartment, learn a little more about her from seeing what she found important in her life.

Knowing almost to the minute how long it would take before she phoned, he checked on the girls and headed for his bedroom. He noticed the unmade bed. He should have at least pulled the covers up that morning. What had Lottie thought when she saw it?

He looked at the computer. The desk was immaculate. She'd stacked his papers in one corner, probably to give herself space to spread out her own. Loosening his tie, he crossed to the chair and touched it lightly, trying to envision her working here. He could imagine her serious expression as she became caught up in the work. He'd noticed it once or twice over the years she'd worked for him.

Could he detect a faint hint of roses? Closing his eyes, he remembered their trip to New York. It seemed like a lifetime ago instead of only days.

By the time the requested call came, he had climbed into bed, conscious all at once of how big it was, and how lonely.

"I'm home safe."

He smiled in the dark. He liked the sound of her voice. Soft and lilting.

"Good. I forgot to ask if you were able to get any work done today."

"Yes, I managed a good two hours while they napped.

Then when they went to bed, I finished up. Actually, with no one around to interrupt, I got a lot done. Nothing along the line of getting that Moran Group contract signed, however. You must feel so proud about that."

"I'm pleased, I have to admit. We worked long and hard, and I'm sure our projections are going to be right on the money."

"I better go. You should get to bed."

"I'm already in bed."

There was a long pause. Asher wished he could see her expression.

"You are?" she said at last

"Six a.m. comes mighty early. And that seems to be the time Madison loves to run and jump in my bed."

"With Kennedy right behind, I imagine."

Asher chuckled. "They surprised me to death that first morning. It was as awkward as could be, too. I used to sleep nude. I wasn't sure if I was ever getting out of bed that day."

Charlotte's soft laughter floated across the telephone line.

Asher tightened his grip on the receiver. He wished she'd stayed a bit longer tonight. He enjoyed talking with her.

And he suspected he'd just shocked her.

"So what did you do?" she asked.

"Tricked them into running to their room to get a book. Then I dashed from the bed, grabbed some jeans and barely made it to the bathroom before they came back. They're as quick as greased lightning, you know."

"I know. So now you chastely wear pajamas?"

"Just the bottoms. I get too hot in bed to wear a top. They're fascinated by my chest hair."

The silence on the other end was telling. Asher smiled again.

"Lottie? What are you thinking?"

It came in a rush.

"Actually I'm thinking this is a totally inappropriate conversation to be having with my boss and that I had better stop before I melt into a puddle, and that I can imagine the twins' fascination. I'd probably share it. Oh, no. I have to go."

She cut the connection.

Interesting reaction. She couldn't be as immune as he'd suspected.

He placed the phone gently on the night stand. Then cradled his head in his stacked hands, gazing up in the dark. Interesting woman, Lottie Thompson.

She hadn't said that! Please, someone tell her she hadn't admitted to sharing the twins' fascination with Asher's chest hair. Heat flooded her cheeks.

She'd never be able to face him. Tomorrow she'd fax in her resignation, cancel the trip this weekend and screen her calls forever.

She dragged herself to the bedroom and changed into her light cotton nightie. As she washed her face, she gazed in the mirror, not surprised to see the heightened color in her cheeks. She could almost die of embarrassment. How could she be so dumb? He was probably laughing himself sick over her naive reaction.

"You are a class-A idiot," she said. "The man is drop-dead gorgeous, but you don't have to act like a teenager with a crush. Besides, he's looking for a wife to watch those children. With a history of marrying for expediency, what else could you expect?"

Not that she was interested in marriage. She had a career to build. She wanted to become secure in her life, prove to herself and the world that she could take care of herself and make a difference.

It would be a long time before she was interested in marriage.

When Charlotte slipped beneath the covers, she couldn't help but remember the big bed in Asher's room. Knowing he slept on the left side seemed very intimate. She bet no one else in the entire firm knew that about him.

Maybe what she said hadn't been so bad. Maybe she could keep working for Callahan Associates. She wasn't sure she could live with Asher withdrawal.

Someone had heard her plea, she thought the next morning when she overheard two fellow employees mention that Asher would be absent yet again. They commiserated with his difficulties in finding competent domestic help.

While sorry he hadn't found a nanny, Charlotte was grateful for the respite. At least she didn't have to face him at work after her embarrassing remark. With any luck she'd come down with the flu before tomorrow morning and have a good excuse to cancel the weekend.

But Saturday dawned clear and sunny, and despite herself, Charlotte felt wonderful. She had to admit to the excitement that filled her at the thought of spending the weekend with

Asher, even going as a nanny for his twins.

She knew she'd spend most of the day in his company. And tonight they were going to dinner alone. She felt almost giddy with anticipation.

She packed a dressy dress, one of the few she owned. It looked a lot more feminine than her business suits. She hoped it'd be appropriate for the restaurant. With a little lace at the collar and cuffs, it was very feminine and she loved wearing it.

Watching from her window, she spotted the three of them when they turned the corner and walked toward her building. Charlotte knew parking was difficult so close to Coit Tower and wondered how far away he'd had to park. The twins were each clinging to a hand, Madison talking nonstop. Kennedy looked around as if absorbing every new sight.

But Charlotte's gaze stayed on Asher. He looked incredibly sexy in jeans and a dark pullover shirt. His hair was tousled, as if the wind had danced through. He laughed at something Madison said and Charlotte's heart clutched. She could look at him all day and never get her fill.

Swallowing hard, she wondered if she were out of her mind to spend the weekend with them.

When the bell rang, she opened her door wide.

"Hi," she said.

Afraid to meet Asher's eyes after her confession on the phone the other night, she smiled at the twins instead.

"Hi, Lottie."

Madison flung herself at Charlotte, wrapping her arms around her legs. Charlotte stooped and hugged the little girls, first Madison, then Kennedy. That ritual complete, the twins darted into the living room and began exploring.

"Don't touch anything," Asher roared.

Charlotte laughed and met his eyes.

"They can't hurt anything here."

"Maybe not, but it's good practice, right?"

She nodded. Her smile began to fade as her awareness of the man in front of her rose.

He stepped closer, his hand cupping the back of her neck. Slowly he smiled that wicked smile.

"I might be equally fascinated," he said in a low drawl.

His free hand took hers and placed it against his chest.

Charlotte blushed to the roots of her hair as his mouth descended over hers.

6

When Asher pulled away, Charlotte kept her eyes closed. She knew this time she was about to die of embarrassment.

"Lottie?"

His voice should be patented, she thought. If they could bottle it and sell it, someone would make millions.

"What?"

She tried to lower her head, her eyes tightly shut, but his finger beneath her chin kept it raised.

"Open your eyes."

She shook her head.

"Why not?"

His tone sounded reasonable.

Why couldn't she feel reasonable?

"Because if I keep my eyes shut, no one can see me."

He laughed. "Like the girls. I don't want to shatter your beliefs, but I can see you. And feel you."

She opened her eyes and found herself gazing directly into his, only a few inches away. Her hands were pressed against his strong chest. Even through the soft cotton covering him, she could feel the hard muscles, the crinkling of hair.

He leaned closer and whispered in her ear, "I will let you look at my chest if I can look at yours."

Dropping her forehead against his shoulder, Charlotte knew she was lost. There was no way out of this quagmire of embarrassment.

"I might as well die now," she moaned.

His chuckle annoyed her.

Was she merely someone to amuse him?

"I, for one, hope you don't. Come on, it's a beautiful day and we have two wild girls to corral and get into the car. It took me fifteen minutes to figure out the car seats. Trying to get one in while the other is loose becomes a real challenge. I should have hired the limo."

He tilted her face once more, brushed his lips across hers and released her.

"Madison, Kennedy, what are you doing?" Asher called.

"Noffing."

"Oh, dear," Charlotte said, spinning.

She knew that tone. *Nothing* always meant something they weren't supposed to be doing. She rushed into her living room, but didn't see them. She moved to the kitchen and stopped in the doorway. Asher pushed against her to peer over her shoulder.

Both twins sat in the middle of the floor, with bread scattered in every direction. Kennedy was attempting to spread a huge chunk of butter on one slice, but the cube was entirely too large to fit on one slice of bread even if it had been soft enough to spread. Crumbs scattered as she pushed the butter into the soft center and through to the floor.

"That's naughty."

Asher set Charlotte aside and strode into the room, frowning at the girls. He stooped and took the butter gingerly from Kennedy's fingers.

"I told you not to touch anything, didn't I?"

Both girls nodded solemnly, their eyes wide with apprehension.

"You have made a mess of Lottie's nice kitchen, wasted food and did it all without permission. Pick up the bread and tell Lottie you're sorry."

Madison's little face drooped with sadness.

"Sorry, Lottie," she said.

Kennedy's thumb shot into her mouth, and her eyes filled with tears.

"Sorry, Lottie."

"Your daddy is right. That was naughty. I think five minutes of time out is appropriate."

She took each child by the hand and drew them to the small table and chairs she used for eating. She placed a child in each chair and admonished them to sit still until the time was up. Turning, she caught Asher dumping the bread in the trash.

"Time out?" he asked, raising one eyebrow.

"They have to sit on those chairs for five minutes, no talking, no getting down and running around."

Charlotte reached for the kitchen timer, set it for five minutes and placed it on the table between the girls.

"Remember, no talking until this bell rings. Next time your daddy tells you not to touch anything, you mind him."

Both girls solemnly nodded, Kennedy still sucking her thumb.

Asher followed Charlotte out of the kitchen.

"I think they're sorry. Isn't five minutes a bit harsh?" he

asked, looking over his shoulder at the forlorn little girls.

She shook her head.

"It might seem endless for them at two, but they have to learn to follow your instructions. This wasn't such a big deal. But if you tell them not to play in the street and they disobey, they could be seriously injured or killed. They have to follow your directions."

"I bow to your superior knowledge and experience."

"You're just glad someone else was around to help with the discipline."

"I am. They are so tiny and young."

"But they need guidance and direction. Don't spoil them, Asher."

"I wouldn't think of it. Are you about ready to leave?"

"Yes."

Her small case sat by the door.

"Wouldn't your hair be more comfortable if you didn't keep it in that braid?" he asked. "This is the weekend, and we're supposed to be having fun."

Charlotte touched the neat braid.

"You don't like it?"

Asher's fingers tangled with hers as he released the band at the base and began to undo the braid.

"I like your hair swirling around your face, resting on your shoulders, looking like a dark cloud with traces of light shining through. And—" he paused and drew her glasses from her nose "—I like you without your glasses."

Charlotte made a grab for the glasses, but he held them out of her reach.

"I need them to see," she protested.

He held them up and looked through them, frowning. "They're not very strong."

She captured them.

"They make the difference between blurry and clear for distances."

"But not close up?" he asked, coming nearer.

Stepping back, she shook her head.

Asher deliberately took another step forward, almost laughing as she stepped back again. He could advance until she ran into the wall. Then what would she do?

"Asher," she began, raising one hand as if to stop him.

The bell sounded on the kitchen timer.

"Daddy!" Madison hollered.

"Saved by the bell," he murmured, tapping Charlotte on her chin and turning to the twins.

Charlotte took a shaky breath as she watched him walk into the kitchen. Her heart pounded as if she'd been in a race. Her tummy fluttered, and her skin tingled. What if the timer hadn't rung? Would he have kissed her?

She was getting entirely too enchanted with those kisses.

Asher carried her small case when they left the apartment. Charlotte held on to the children. They skipped beside her and chattered about visiting Grandpa.

"Do they understand the concept?" Asher asked.

"I'm sure they don't. They probably think it's his name. This is mine."

He stopped by a late-model sedan. The rich dark burgundy color was complemented by a pale gray interior. In the back seat were two car seats. He opened the door and reached for Kennedy when Madison scrambled in. Charlotte made short work of getting the girls settled. Five minutes later they were off.

"Nice car," she murmured, rubbing her fingertips along the leather seat.

Soft and pristine. She wondered how long he'd had it.

"I don't use it much. Around town I usually take a cab, or lately the limo. But it's great for long trips, comfortable."

"I'd have expected a sports car."

"I had one when we first showed a profit. But they take a lot of care to keep them performance tuned. This is more convenient."

"Tell me something about your grandfather," Charlotte said.

"What's to tell? He's eighty-three, a crusty old man. He's lived alone since my grandmother died when my dad was in high school—except for raising me. His house is old and doesn't have much to recommend it."

"But he's family," she said softly. "I bet he'll be crazy about these little girls."

"Maybe. He's going to be surprised."

"As you were. Did you ever find a reason your wife didn't tell you about them?"

"None that is conclusive. She didn't leave a letter confessing all, if that's what you mean. But her attorney suggested she was afraid I'd insist she stay home and play mommy instead of working. Sarah thinks that's probably the case, as well. Addie was obsessed with the business world. She wanted to become a big player in a big field."

"And what do you want, Asher?"

"I want to have a successful company. I enjoy the

challenge of getting new business and keeping it. But Callahan Associates is already doing great. I don't want to grow so large I lose all control."

"What else do you want to do with life?"

He flicked her a look then returned his attention to the road.

"Funny you should ask that. A month ago I would have said more of the same. But with Addie dying so unexpectedly and finding out I'm a father, I've been doing some thinking. I'm not sure what I want, but my life has already changed tremendously. I'm thinking of finding a nice house for the girls, investing in college accounts. What do you want?"

"A chance to be myself. I love working at Callahan Associates. I'm doing a good job with my accounts. The World vision project is tremendous. I expect to pull off a stellar success. Then I want to discuss a serious increase in responsibilities and salary."

He laughed.

"Always with an eye to the main chance."

"Isn't that the business way?"

"What about your personal life? I take it you don't have a serious relationship going."

He'd kissed her silly more times than she could keep track of and he only brought that up now?

"No, I don't."

"No distractions while you work your way to the top?"

"Something like that."

Kennedy demanded a story. Charlotte was relieved to turn in her seat to comply. It ended the uncomfortable trend of their conversation.

It was just past noon when they reached Sonora. They'd had to stop twice for rest breaks and to give the girls a few minutes to run around.

The awkward tension eased and Charlotte relaxed and began to enjoy herself. She'd never been in this part of the state and was fascinated to see how different the Sierra Nevada mountains were from the barren mountains around Los Angeles. Tall pines and firs soared toward a crystalline blue sky. The air was redolent with the scent of the cedar and pines—fresh and clean.

Asher turned into a long graveled driveway and stopped near an old house. It needed paint but looked solid except for that.

An old man came to the door, peering out to see who had arrived. His face softened when he recognized Asher.

"Hello, Grandpa."

Asher greeted the older man, then turned to open the car door. He unfastened Kennedy while Charlotte released Madison from the other side. He wondered what the old man would think of his daughters.

Suddenly proud of them, he wanted his grandfather to love them as much as he did.

He took Kennedy in his arms, picked up the big white bag from the seat, turned and walked toward the house.

"I hope it was all right to drop by. I should have called."

Charlotte followed him, watching avidly as the older man looked at Asher, then the two girls and finally her.

"This is your home, boy, come any time. I see you brought guests. Howdy, ma'am."

"This is Charlotte Thompson. She works for me. Lottie, my grandfather, Silas Callahan," Asher said. "And these two young ladies are Madison and Kennedy Callahan. My daughters."

The old man started, then gazed fiercely at the little girls.

"Looks like you might have mentioned something before today," he said gruffly.

"I only found out myself a week ago. Let's go inside and I'll explain everything. We stopped at the burger place in town and brought lunch. I hope you haven't eaten."

Asher lifted the bag.

"Not yet. Come in, Miss Thompson."

"Charlotte, please," she said, stepping onto the porch and putting Madison down.

"Or Lottie, like we call her," Asher said.

The two little girls cautiously entered the dark house.

"Now you young 'uns don't be getting into anything," Grandpa admonished.

They looked at him with wide eyes and didn't move.

"Hmm. I think I have the blocks your daddy played with when he was a little boy. Where did I put them?"

By the time lunch had ended the girls seemed right at home with Silas Callahan. As Charlotte had predicted, he was charmed with the twins.

"I thought I'd take Lottie to Columbia. She's never been to the gold country before," Asher said. "The girls need to nap. Can I leave them with you while we go?"

"I don't know anything about watching little girls. Boys I could handle."

Charlotte smiled.

"They don't need much watching when they sleep. And you've been perfect with them so far. I think they are delighted with their great-grandfather."

"Never thought I'd see the day. Not after that dang fool marriage of yours. I guess it wasn't always platonic."

Asher looked uncomfortable but shrugged, obviously used to his grandfather's blunt ways.

Once the girls were asleep, he and Charlotte took off.

Charlotte thoroughly enjoyed her afternoon in Columbia. Fascinated by the old town, she stopped to read every placard and asked innumerable questions. Surprisingly, Asher seemed to know the answer to every one.

"How do you know so much, or are you making it up?" she asked.

He laughed and threaded his fingers through hers, pulling her to the next historical sign.

"I grew up around here, remember. You can't live in the gold country without absorbing the history. The California gold rush was one of the largest migration of people in history. Men came from all over the world in hopes of finding color. And I have to admit, it's just as fascinating today as it was when I was growing up. I used to hike down to the Stanislaus River and pan for gold hoping to find a huge nugget or maybe a lost vein somewhere."

"Did you ever get any color?" she asked, feeling almost like a true Argonaut using the jargon.

"A few flakes. I still have them in a jar at Grandpa's. Not enough to set the world on fire."

"Could we go panning?"

"Sure, there's a place here in town. They salt the sand, charge tourists a few bucks and everyone is guaranteed to find some gold."

"I'd rather take the chance in the river."

"We'll do it some day. Maybe we'll still find the mother lode. What would you do with a ton of money?"

"Start my own business," Charlotte said promptly.

Then she looked up.

"Oh, not that I don't love working at Callahan Associates. But I'd like to be running things one day."

"What would you change about the company if you could?" he asked as if truly interested.

"I don't know enough about the entire setup to suggest any major changes. I know I have a lot to learn. But I have ideas and want to see how they work at some point. It will be years before I'm ready to run an organization. But if I came into a gold mine, then I could hire competent help like you do."

"So you'd be my competition."

Charlotte stopped and thought about it for a moment.

"I guess so, in a way. But by the time I'm ready to do anything, Callahan Associates will be a huge firm and I'll start small—going for the little guys who can't afford you."

"Sentiment like that won't make you big bucks."

"But money isn't that important—knowing you can succeed at the job is what counts. Don't you think?"

"I work for a number of reasons. Money is one of them. But the satisfaction I get is a greater one," Asher admitted.

"But you still want that gold mine?" Charlotte teased.

"Yeah, I still do."

Charlotte didn't get her dinner out that night. When they reached Silas's home, he'd already started a huge pot of beef stew. When he learned of their plans he looked so crestfallen that Charlotte immediately told Asher they should eat with him and the girls.

"But I planned to take you to the hotel. They have wonderful food and a small combo on the weekends for dancing."

"Take her another time, boy. I want to hear more about what's going on in your life and what you're planning to do with these young 'uns," Silas said. "Besides, it's one thing to watch these angels while they sleep. I suspect they are as full of mischief as you were at that age when awake."

"Tell him about the makeup," Charlotte suggested, settling in one of the comfortable chairs.

She felt wonderful.

The afternoon had passed so swiftly she could hardly believe it. It was because of her companion, she knew. He'd been attentive and informative and fun. And she'd discovered a bit more about her boss. Asher was a fascinating man.

"It's all tied in with trying to get a nanny," Asher began.

Silas chuckled at the antics of the twins and twice threw speculative glances at Charlotte.

"Looks to me like you ought to think about getting married again," he said when Asher finished.

She pretended to not notice. The last thing she needed

was for Asher to get the idea that she would be the perfect wife. He'd mentioned it a couple of times—always right after she helped with the twins.

Dinner was lively. The girls constantly tried to dominate the conversation. They were intrigued with the older man and loved chatting with him. He nodded and smiled and acted as if he understood every word. They were enchanted.

When the dishes had been washed and put away, without the girls' help this time, they all sat in the living room. Kennedy snuggled into Asher's lap and Madison hesitated, torn between her newly discovered great-grandfather and Lottie. Finally, she wandered to Lottie and raised her arms.

"Up."

Charlotte pulled her into her lap and hugged her. These girls were so precious. For a moment she gave a thought to their mother. Addie would miss so much.

"That tale you told earlier about the makeup reminded me of the time you got into the honey, remember?" Silas said, leaning back in his chair, a look of amusement covering his face.

"No need to rake up old stories, Grandpa," Asher said hastily.

Charlotte laughed.

"We girls would love to hear it, wouldn't we, Madison?"

When she nodded vigorously, Silas began telling tales about Asher as a little boy. It was obvious the girls weren't too sure who the little boy was. They kept looking at their father. He was so big, it must be impossible for them to imagine him as a small child.

Charlotte reveled in each story, intrigued with the

glimpses into Asher's past.

His life had been quite different from hers. He'd found love and security with his grandfather. He was so lucky.

She had a box full of mementos from various homes and her cherished dolly—that was all.

No one to sit with and reminisce.

The conversation centered around Asher's antics as a boy, and from the fond way his grandfather told the tales, the old man clearly loved his only grandson.

When Kennedy fell asleep in his arms, Asher rose to put her to bed.

"I'll be back for that one," he said.

Charlotte started to rise, but Silas shook his head. When Asher had left, he turned to her.

"Let him do it. I wanted a chance to talk with you, and this is probably the only one I'll get. Never saw my boy so attentive to someone before. He never lets you take six steps away."

Charlotte flushed.

"I don't think that's quite so. I'm here to help with the girls."

"It's about the girls, I'm thinking. He needs a wife. Someone to help him raise these young'uns. You seem to know what you're doing. Ever have children?"

"In a manner of speaking. I watched children while I was growing up—after school, weekends, nights."

"Mmm, it shows. You've got a good touch with these little girls. From what I heard today, better even than their mother."

He shook his head.

"Dang fool idea marrying to start a business. Yet it seemed to work. The firm is doing well, if Asher's reports are true. But now Asher needs someone to show him how to make a family. We didn't have a normal one. No woman in the place."

Silas chuckled suddenly.

"That's sure not the case here—he's already outnumbered. A wife would only add to the female majority."

Charlotte smiled politely.

"Don't you think Asher should marry for love?" she asked. "Not just to acquire another wife?"

"Don't know if it'll ever happen. Sometimes being a good companion is all you can expect. I had that with Emma. Asher's father fell in love with his wife and they fought like cats and dogs. I don't know that I believe love is necessary for a marriage. More important things come into play."

Charlotte felt Madison fall asleep, her body suddenly limp and heavy. She cuddled her closer, breathing in her sweet baby scent.

Maybe Asher could be excused for his first marriage, if his grandfather's advice was anything to go by. But he'd be doing himself and his new wife a disservice if he married again without love.

Did he even know what it was? How to display it?

Of course he did. He was loving and devoted to his children—and he'd learned of their existence less than two weeks ago.

For a second she wished he'd show her the same affection, come to care for her as strongly as he obviously cared for his daughters.

But she knew the folly of such wishful thinking.

"One down, now for number two," Asher said, crossing the room to lift Madison from Charlotte's lap. His dark eyes gazed into hers, and she almost lifted her hand to his cheek. Clenching her fingers, she looked away, right into the wise eyes of Silas Callahan.

He looked quickly at his grandson and then gazed into space, but Charlotte wasn't fooled. The old man wanted something to develop between them. It didn't matter to him if they loved one another. He wanted someone to help his grandson.

Asher hesitated in the doorway on his way back to the living room. The girls were both sound asleep. It was still early enough that he and Charlotte could run down to the hotel and have dessert, maybe dance for a while.

Except for the plane ride to New York and the afternoon in Columbia, they'd never spent any time together without the girls. He'd looked forward to this evening.

She'd left her hair down after he'd released it that morning. In the afternoon's sun it had glowed like rich ebony. She looked young and carefree and delighted with every tidbit he shared. Soaking up the folklore from gold rush days, she'd questioned him incessantly. Just like the twins did. Only he had an easier time talking with Charlotte.

Easier than with most of the women he knew.

Watching her from the shadows in the hall, he wondered why. She chatted with his grandfather. He could hear the murmur of their voices, but not the words. From the comments his not-so-sly grandfather made, Asher knew Silas thought Charlotte would make the perfect wife for a widower with two small children.

Sometimes Asher thought so himself.

Would she consent to marry him? It would solve so marry problems if she'd many him and be a stay-at-home wife.

He shook his head. To look at, she seemed like the perfect mate, sweet and docile. But he knew she'd never agree to such a plan. Her career was too important to her.

His eyes hardened. How did women put mere business ahead of caring for their children? Wasn't there joy and excitement in raising a child? Shaping how they'd face the future?

First Addie, now Charlotte. Neither wanted to raise children. Each wanted to make it in business.

Yet didn't he want the same thing? He didn't plan to stay home with the children. It was the old double standard. In an instant he realized how Charlotte felt.

But even if she didn't stay home, she'd be there in the evenings, giving advice, telling him how to handle discipline and giving the girls a different perspective. Children needed a mother and a father. It was up to him to provide both for his twins.

"Are they asleep?" Charlotte asked when he stepped into the living room.

"Never even stirred when I put them in their pajamas. I think they'll sleep through until morning."

He looked at Silas.

"It's still early. Would you watch them while Charlotte and

I head for town?"

"Sure. Asleep I can handle them."

"How about it, Lottie, want to go out for dessert?"

"I don't know, Asher. I thought we could sit here and have Silas share more of his memories. Think of the blackmail I can use with all I'm learning," she teased.

"I see I need to get a vow of silence from you before we leave," Asher replied, sitting on the chair opposite her.

"It's still warm out. Want to go for a walk?"

"That I'd like." Charlotte jumped up.

"We'll be back soon, Silas. Dust off all those old stories."

Charlotte stopped abruptly on the porch. Asher ran into her.

"Whoops," he said, stopping suddenly. "What's wrong?"

"It's so dark here. In the city there are streetlights, lights from all the buildings. It's black as pitch here."

"Give your eyes a chance to get used to the dark. The stars provide light. And once the moon gets above the trees, we'll be able to see fine. I know my way around, Lottie. Come on."

He took her hand in his, threaded his fingers through hers and stepped off the porch. Walking in the center of the graveled drive, Asher kept his pace slow to make it easier on Lottie. She was as high as his shoulder. Her stride was short.

"It's quiet here, too," she murmured as they strolled down the drive.

When they reached the country road, he turned left.

"It must have been so much fun to grow up here. Did you have a tree fort?"

"Sure. And swings hanging from tree limbs. We used to

swim at one of the creeks that feed the Stan."

"No wonder you want to get a house with a yard for your girls."

"And a mother."

Asher stopped and pulled Lottie in front of him. His hands rested on her shoulders as he lowered his head, trying to see her in the dim light.

"Will you provide them with that, Lottie? Will you marry me?"

7

Charlotte stared at him in dawning horror. She pulled free, turned and walked briskly along the path they'd just taken. She'd run if she could. Instead she had to settle for furiously stomping, trying to see in the faint illumination from the stars.

"Lottie, wait a minute."

Asher reached for her arm and stopped her.

"At least discuss it," he said.

"What's to discuss? I won't be a nanny or childcare provider for the rest of my life. I spent a lot of time and effort to get a business degree so I could move beyond that. I want to use it."

"I never said you couldn't use your degree, that I didn't want you to work. But you're so good with the girls. They like you. You like them. It would be the perfect solution."

"For you, maybe. I don't see it in any way perfect."

"You want to get married some day, don't you? Most women do. We get along. We had a good time today—"

"Asher, stop. Just because we had fun one afternoon doesn't mean we're suited for *marriage*. Listen to yourself. You couldn't even make a pretense of wanting me for myself. All you want is a mother for the girls. A woman doesn't want to be married unless she's loved and cherished. Or at the very least appreciated for herself. We don't even know each other."

"You've worked for me for two years. I know how you are in the office, and these last couple of weeks I've seen how you are with the girls. We have the foundation for a strong marriage. And I've never lied to you. Did you want me to fall on my knees and declare my undying love?"

His scathing tone displayed his feelings.

"No. You wouldn't mean it."

"You're right. I don't believe in love, at least not the fairy-tale version. But we could build a good life together. Don't say no tonight, Lottie. Think about it."

"I don't need to think about it. I—"

Before Charlotte could finish her sentence, Asher covered her mouth with his.

It was as if she had been waiting especially for his touch. Her lips parted, and he took advantage, tracing the soft flesh with his tongue, slipping inside to sip of her sweetness.

He moved his hands to the silky softness of her hair, to hold her close and positioned for his kiss. He forgot the burden of becoming a sudden father, forgot about the demands of the office. The only reality was the petite woman in his arms and the fire her kisses fed.

At last he pulled back and gazed at her bemused expression. A skilled negotiator, Asher knew when to keep silent. He wanted her and he hoped to marry her. But sometimes pushing too hard could kill a deal.

He'd coax her, cajole her and bribe her, if need be. But he wanted her for the mother of his daughters, and he'd do his best to bring that about.

"Let's return to the house. I don't think you want a walk,"

he said, releasing her. "We'll talk more about this later."

He was careful to stay near but did not touch her on the walk back. The light on the porch beckoned and Charlotte increased her pace when she saw it.

"I don't need to talk further," she said as she mounted the steps to the wide porch.

She'd kept quiet on the walk back, too stunned at the turn of events to marshal her thoughts. But she wanted to make her position clear before retiring for the night.

"And I won't take no for an answer tonight. Go on inside, I still want a walk."

Asher waited until she was at the door, then spun and headed toward the road.

Charlotte watched him stride away, her heart fluttering wildly in her chest. His kiss had been devastating. She'd have fallen in a heap if he hadn't been holding her. Her knees had felt like marshmallows.

Lightly she brushed her warm lips with her fingertips. If she was foolish enough to ever entertain his notion of marriage, she'd be entitled to kisses like that all the time.

With a quiet groan, she opened the door. She'd never get anything done if that were the case. Asher's kisses disturbed her too much to promote clear thinking.

Charlotte spent some time visiting with Silas. He spoke of Sonora and the changes he'd seen in the sleepy little gold rush town during the years he'd lived there. Before long his eyes began to droop, and Charlotte knew he was growing tired.

"I think I'll just slip on to bed, if that's all right," she said, standing.

When he nodded, she crossed the hall to the spare room

that had been assigned to her. The bed wasn't large, but more than ample. She was glad she'd brought a long cotton nightgown. The evenings in the mountains were cool.

Turning off the lights a little while later, Charlotte lay awake in the dark listening for Asher's step.

She tried to ignore the churning of her senses as she relived his proposal. No mention of love or devotion. Simply that his girls needed a mother and he wanted her for the job. Was that how he saw a wife—as someone to fill a position like any employee?

She wanted to be angry at the callous way he phrased things. But she couldn't help imagining being married to him. Seeing him every day and every night. Sharing meals, bath time with the twins and family outings.

She rolled on her side and curled up the way she had as a child. Was she foolish to pass up his proposal? She'd admired him since the day they'd met.

Since finding out his wife had died, her feelings had become stronger. Not that admiration was a foundation for marriage. Ever since her mother had died, she'd searched for love. Should she settle for anything less?

What would happen when she refused? He'd turn to someone else, of course. His interest in her was tied to the twins. He'd never looked at her twice before insisting she accompany him on the trip to New York and she'd only been pressed into service for that journey because she had crucial experience.

In all fairness, she had to admit, prior to that he'd been a married man. He was too honorable to have shown any interest in a woman not his wife. Given the circumstances of his marriage, she thought even more highly of him that he hadn't sought other women.

Would he be as loyal to her as he had been to Addie? How could he propose another business affair?

But then, from the stories she'd heard tonight about his childhood, what did Asher know about a family? His parents had evidently fought every moment of their marriage. When they died, he'd moved in with his crusty old grandfather. Silas had admitted his wife had been the primary parent with their son. He'd had limited experience when it came to raising Asher.

Charlotte smiled in the dark. She thought the old man had done a wonderful job. Asher was kind and considerate. A bit arrogant and demanding, but that could be excused or worked around. The honesty and honor that shone so strongly were not traits to be learned, but innate.

She could do worse.

What was she doing—considering his ludicrous proposal? Couldn't she do better?

Couldn't she find a man who loved her?

She had to refuse Asher. Her career was important.

And somewhere, some time, there'd be someone who loved her.

The steps in the hall were quiet, but Charlotte recognized them. Asher was safe at home. Curiously content, she drifted to sleep.

The next morning Charlotte came awake when her door opened. Two thumping sets of feet crossed the room and two small bodies flung themselves against the side of her bed. Opening her eyes slowly, she gazed into identical sunny faces.

"Hi, there," Charlotte said, smiling.

They looked adorable.

"Hi, Lottie. Up?" Madison held up her arms.

"Me, too," said Kennedy.

Charlotte drew both girls into the bed, snuggling one on either side of her. Their bare feet were freezing. She tucked the blankets around the three of them and settled against the pillow, her heart singing.

"Tell us a story," Madison demanded.

Charlotte hid a smile. The child sounded as imperious as her father. Her heart filled with love for these precious twin girls. They looked so alike yet were so different.

"How about Jack and the Beanstalk?" Charlotte asked.

She launched into the tale, stretching out scenes, using a gruff voice for the giant, saying, "Fee, fie, fo, fum."

They watched her with rapt attention, giggling at the silly parts, looking mesmerized when the giant began to pursue Jack.

"Isn't that a little scary for two-year-olds?" Asher asked from the door.

Charlotte looked up, startled. She'd been so engrossed in entertaining the girls she hadn't heard him. He'd dressed in jeans and a blue cotton shirt. His shoulder propped against the doorjamb, he crossed his arms and watched them.

"It's just a fairy tale. All of them are a bit gruesome and violent. But didn't you hear them when you were little?"

He nodded.

"But I was a boy."

"As if that makes a difference."

"Hi, Daddy." Madison waved. "We snuggle wif Lottie."

"I see you two are snuggled with Lottie. Is there room for me?"

Charlotte's gaze flew to his as color stained her cheeks.

"No, there is not room for you."

"It is a small bed. My king-size bed at home would hold all of us easily."

Charlotte remembered the huge bed that dominated his bedroom, the tousled covers and the indented left pillow. She could sleep on the right side, and when the girls wakened they could join them, snuggling beneath the covers for more storytelling.

The image was so sharp, Charlotte thought she could reach out and touch it. Longing rose.

She could have that life if she said yes.

"Time to get up. Grandpa's making flapjacks," Asher said, eyeing her quizzically.

"What's fap jack?" Kennedy asked, pulling her thumb from her mouth.

"Pancakes, baby girl, the best this side of the Mississippi."

"Well, that frame of reference will help these two," Charlotte said, wishing Asher would leave.

How was she to get out of bed with him standing there watching every move?

He smiled and remained standing exactly where he was.

"Want to get the girls dressed first?" she asked.

"No. I shudder to think how much syrup they'll spill on themselves. We can give them a quick bath after breakfast, throw the nightgowns in the laundry. Did you bring a robe?"

Charlotte nodded. Not that she had any intention of sitting in her nightgown and robe and eating breakfast while

Asher was fully dressed and looking as sexy as could be.

"I'd rather dress before breakfast," she said primly.

"Now, why am I not surprised? Hurry up, then, Grandpa already has the first batch in the pan."

The girls scooted from the bed and raced out the door.

"Get something on their feet. They were like ice when they climbed in with me," Charlotte said, sitting up, holding the blanket.

She felt as shy as a Victorian maiden, but there was no way she was getting out of bed with Asher standing there watching her.

"Need help?"

She glared at him. He knew. Darn him.

"Go help your daughters."

Laughing softly, he pushed away from the door frame. But he didn't head for the kitchen. He stepped into her room, immediately displacing all the air.

Charlotte watched, mesmerized, as he slowly crossed the small space to her bed. Her heart pounded. She couldn't breathe. Her fingers clutched the blanket tightly while she watched his every move. She didn't trust that gleam in his eyes.

"Good morning," he said, and leaned over to kiss her.

Charlotte didn't know how her face tilted to his. She closed her eyes and felt as if she were floating. She was pressed against the pillows before she could draw a breath. And when she did, Asher flooded her senses. How did her arms find their way around his neck? How could she be holding on so tightly? She didn't want to encourage the man. He had enough dangerous ideas without her contributing to them.

"Asher!" Silas roared from the kitchen. "Breakfast is on

the table."

"Uh-oh."

Asher pulled away and sat on the edge of the bed, his fingers brushing the tangle of dark hair on the pillow.

"That's his get-in-here-this-minute voice. I remember it well from when I was growing up."

"Don't you think you'd better go?"

Charlotte wanted to throw herself into his arms and have him kiss her again. Her heated blood rushed through her veins. She could scarcely breathe, and she was practically asking him to stay.

"Are you getting up?"

"Yes, after you leave."

She drew the covers higher and glared at him. "You shouldn't be here."

It was too little, too late, but she tried to draw on some modicum of common sense and practicality.

"I like it here. I like being around you," he said, grinning audaciously.

"The answer is still no."

Defiant, she refused to be cajoled into agreeing to his outrageous proposal.

"I don't remember asking any question."

"The one from last night."

"Ah, that one. I don't want to discuss that yet. Maybe later. Keep an open mind."

"No. I've told you the answer already."

"Charlotte, you're new at negotiating. You haven't heard all the points yet. There's always a price. I just have to find yours."

He took her hand and held it in his, studying it, tracing the soft skin with a fingertip.

"Now you make me sound like a piece of furniture. You're planning to buy me?"

"Maybe bribe?"

Six kisses a day would probably do it, her traitorous mind thought.

Gathering her dignity, she withdrew her hand.

"If you would let me have a little privacy, I'd get up and dressed."

"Don't get dressed on my account."

"You're dressed."

"I can change that."

He reached for the top button of his shirt.

"No!"

She closed her eyes tightly. "Go eat breakfast."

The bed shifted when he rose, and she heard his chuckle as he walked away. He could be very aggravating.

She opened her eyes, flung the covers off, got up, snatched her clothes and headed for the bathroom. The sooner they ate and got on the road, the sooner she'd be home, safe and sound.

And alone.

"I'm not getting married to be a substitute mother," she said to her reflection in the mirror.

She brushed her hair until it shone. Satisfied she looked her best in the comfortable jeans and jonquil-yellow shirt, she tossed her nightgown on the bed and hurried to the kitchen.

No sense abusing Silas's hospitality because of her annoyance with Asher.

"Sleep good?" Silas asked when she appeared in the doorway.

"Great."

Ignoring Asher, she took the seat the older man indicated and looked at the stack of pancakes on her plate.

"I can't eat all this."

Did Silas think she was a lumberjack? There must have been eight or nine huge pancakes.

"Eat what you want. The rest we'll throw out for the birds," Asher said.

"We have fap jacks," Kennedy said.

A trail of glistening syrup on her chin and the front of her nightie indicating she'd started dribbling when she began eating.

"They're vewy good," Madison said around a mouthful.

"Swallow before talking," Charlotte said softly, then darted a glance at Asher.

She'd spoken before thinking. Acting like a mother. She didn't like the smug expression on his face. He was driving her crazy. She'd said no a half dozen times. Wasn't he listening?

Charlotte ate quickly, hoping they could head for home soon. It'd been a mistake to come for the weekend. She needed distance and the sanctity of her apartment to gather her defenses.

And she needed to stay away from Asher. The man wouldn't listen to her. Kissed her whenever it suited him. And she'd told him no.

Well, maybe she hadn't told him not to kiss her again, she admitted. But surely he knew they had no future together.

He should be out looking for another woman to become

the mother of his children.

The thought hit her.

If he found someone else, he'd never kiss her again. Wouldn't call her to help with Madison or Kennedy. Another woman would be charmed by the twins, laugh at their antics, have her heart melt when Kennedy snuggled close and smiled in quiet happiness.

Charlotte would have her career.

Somehow the excitement had faded.

She needed to get home to regain her perspective.

But Asher was in no hurry. Once the girls were cleaned up and dressed, they went outside. He insisted Charlotte join them, then had her suggest the games they play.

"You know what children like," he said, reinforcing her belief he saw her as a child-care specialist only.

The day was beautiful. The sun shone in a cloudless sky. A slight breeze brought the scent of cedar and pine. Warmth from the sun's rays kept them comfortable. A change from the briskness in the air last night.

With the intent of giving them plenty of exercise before the long car ride, Charlotte suggested red light, green light. The girls did their best. If they didn't always stop at red light, no one seemed to care. Laughing and giggling, they ran fast to reach their daddy, who was it.

After several sets, they switched to follow the leader. Madison insisted Lottie lead them. Charlotte hopped, watching as the twins did their best to copy her. Then she pirouetted, then skipped. She ran slowly, then stopped abruptly. Both girls careered into her, then Asher followed.

They all tumbled to the ground, laughing and squirming.

In a flash both girls were on their feet.

"That's fun!" Madison said, beaming at the two adults still on the ground.

"Yeah, well, I wasn't expecting your father," Charlotte said, sitting.

Asher lay back, stacked his hands and rested his head on them.

"I haven't played games like these in more than twenty-five years."

"You never lose your touch. Were you always this klutzy?" she asked, looking at him.

He'd closed his eyes, turned his face toward the sun. His skin was already tanned, taut over high cheekbones. Charlotte wished she dared trace the outlines of his face, feel that warm skin, test the closeness of his shave.

Kennedy plopped down beside Asher.

"No nap," she said, poking him.

He smiled and opened one eye.

"Not napping, just resting."

"Daddy's really old. He needs to rest after he plays," Charlotte said.

"Witch," he said without heat. "You'll have them believing that."

"Daddy old," Kennedy yelled to Madison.

Then she scrambled to her feet and went to see what her twin was doing. Pulling up dandelions, as far as Charlotte could tell. She watched them to make sure they didn't put the flowers in their mouths.

"Thirty-two is not old."

"If you're two, it is."

"How old are you?"

"Twenty-five."

"It would be a real marriage, Lottie. I want to have more children. You could have your own babies as well as these," Asher said without opening his eyes. "Maybe a few years ahead of what you planned, but so what? That just means they'll be grown and gone earlier. You'll still have many years to build a huge career."

She watched the twins as heat washed through her at his words.

Babies with Asher? Maybe a little boy next time? A tough little guy who would like to spend summers visiting with Silas, playing in the mountains, growing up like his daddy.

Charlotte took a shaky breath and stood.

"It's getting late. We should pack up and head back. I think we've run them ragged. They'll probably sleep the entire way home."

"Just to be full of pep when we get back, huh?"

Watching as he effortlessly rose, Charlotte couldn't help but notice how well he filled out his jeans, how his shirt emphasized the broadness of his shoulders. He looked serious in his business suits. Casual clothes revealed the tantalizing masculinity of his body. She closed her eyes and turned away.

"Lottie?" Asher came closer.

"What?"

"It's time to discuss this. And I'm willing to throw in something else. Something that I think will appeal to you."

She looked at him and held her breath. He was so dear to her. Suddenly she knew why she wanted him to kiss her, to spend time with her. To want her—not as a mother to his children but for his own personal lover.

She loved him.

She'd admired him for months, reveled in every hint of praise he'd showed her at work, more so than praise from a boss would normally warrant.

But these last two weeks had shown her how truly special Asher was. He'd taken a bad blow with the unexpected discovery of the twins.

And immediately taken charge.

She could tell by watching them that he adored his daughters.

She wished he felt some of that same adoration for her.

Her heart pounded. She couldn't marry the man—yet how could she allow him to marry anyone else?

Asher leaned toward her, his eyes searching her face. Slowly he drew off her glasses and tucked them in his shirt pocket.

"Marry me, and I'll throw in twenty percent ownership of Callahan Associates. Your career will be assured forever."

Stunned, she stared at him. For a moment she thought she might faint. The trees and deep blue sky faded to a nondescript gray. She could only focus on his dark eyes and the echo of the words that played in her head.

"What did you say?"

"You heard me, twenty percent. Which isn't all bad considering I only have fifty-one percent. The other forty-nine percent now belongs to Madison and Kennedy. It will still be a family organization. And we can vote their stock for another nineteen years or so. What do you say? Is it enough?"

Tears stung her eyes. She'd just realized she loved the

man, and he was bribing her to marry him!

Her heart ached.

Gently Asher tucked a strand of hair behind her ear, his fingers lingering a moment longer than necessary, as if he enjoyed the feel of her soft skin.

"Just like a marketing analyst to analyze everything to death," he said into the growing silence. "Just say yes, Lottie. Don't look for every possible ramification."

"It'll never work."

"Of course it will work," he said arrogantly. "We'll make sure of it. Say yes."

Charlotte held her breath, thoughts spinning in her mind.

Take a chance. She drew a deep breath and threw caution to the wind. Slowly she nodded.

Asher smiled and leaned forward as if to kiss her. She raised her face. She was probably making the biggest mistake of her life, but recklessly throwing caution to the wind, she promised herself she'd do all she could to make sure it did work.

His breath brushed across her cheeks. Closing her eyes, she waited for his kiss.

"Madison, no!"

Asher's voice roared in her ear. He released her and he darted to the little girl, then he thrust his finger inside her mouth and popped out mangled dandelion petals. He stooped and scolded the child.

Charlotte watched, the scene slightly blurry. Engaged eight seconds and already he'd ignored her for his children. Was this a sign of how their life would be?

Not if she could help it. But she'd better make sure he

never suspected she'd fallen in love with him. He was the type to take advantage of that fact.

The drive home was quiet. The twins fell asleep in their car seats almost as soon as Asher pulled away from his grandfather's house. Silas had packed them a picnic lunch, but Charlotte refused to let Asher waken the girls. They were tired and could use the sleep. And it would make the trip to San Francisco go that much faster if they made no stops.

Her mind spun in a million directions. She had some more work to do on the World vision account before they could finalize their preliminary draft.

Had Melanie finished her part of the projections? Charlotte would check first thing in the morning. After work tomorrow, she needed to get some groceries.

She tried to keep her mind from the monumental change she'd agreed to, but she couldn't do so for long.

If they married, she wouldn't need her apartment anymore. Could she get a sublet? The thought crashed into her.

She'd agreed to marry Asher Callahan.

Was she making a mistake?

Darting a glance at him, she wondered how soon he'd want to get married. Could she really go through with this? Wasn't it too soon after his wife's death?

If she didn't, he'd find someone else. That above all else reinforced her decision.

He flicked a glance at her.

"Having second thoughts?" he asked calmly.

"Maybe."

He frowned.

"I thought we could be married next Friday. I'll have Sarah set things up at the courthouse. We'll get the license one day this week at lunch."

"So soon?"

Panic threatened to flare.

"Any reason to wait?" Asher asked reasonably.

Charlotte shook her head. She'd get used to this. She hoped.

"You don't think it's too soon after Addie's death? She was your wife and hasn't even been dead a month."

"You know as well as everyone in the company that we hadn't seen each other in almost a year. Ours was a marriage to build the business. I expected one day one of us would ask for a divorce to marry someone else."

"Someone you loved?"

"Or if she fell in love. Anyway, it's no one's business but ours."

Asher bypassed her apartment and drove directly to his. She helped feed the children supper and then bathed them. For a few moments she felt as if she'd been transported back to New York, taking care of the girls, feeling awkward and out of place in the apartment. Only now the routine was growing familiar.

Sweet-smelling and ready for bed, the girls ran to the living room to bounce on the sofa, ready for a story.

"Lottie can tell us the story," Asher said as he scooped up Madison and held her in his lap.

When Charlotte sat, he scooted over until his hip touched

hers, his thigh pressed against hers. His look dared her to object.

Scarcely able to breathe, much less concentrate on a story, Charlotte cuddled close with Kennedy and held out her hand to Madison.

"Do fee fum," the little girl demanded, placing her hand in Charlotte's and smiling winningly.

Despite their long nap, both girls were nodding by the time Charlotte finished her rendition of Jack and the Beanstalk. She and Asher carried the twins into their room and tucked them into their cribs.

For the first time Charlotte considered what she'd agreed to. She'd have an instrumental role in shaping the lives of these precious children. She'd be the mommy they remembered. She'd be the one to take them to school, attend their Christmas plays, hear their lessons and mop up tears when they were teenagers and boys proved perplexing and disappointing.

And she knew she'd love them both until the day she died. Just as she loved their father.

Turning, she smiled shyly at Asher.

"This is the best time."

"They are angels when asleep, aren't they?"

He led the way to the living room.

"Are you anxious to be off or can you stay and talk for a few minutes?" he asked.

"I can stay if you want me to," she said.

He studied her.

"Sounds like the perfect employee. You're a partner now, Lottie. And in less than a week you'll be my wife."

"And what do you expect of this marriage, Asher? For me to meekly bow to your will?"

He laughed.

"Not from you. I expect you'll do whatever you think is right and let me know somewhere along the way."

Unexpectedly his face sobered. He drew her closer and rested his forehead against hers.

"I'm expecting a willing wife. A woman who will help me with the children and with the business. I don't expect you to stay at home and devote yourself to Madison and Kennedy. But you'll be here every night and weekends. As much as I will."

"And for yourself?" she asked, wishing he'd stop talking and kiss her so soundly she never had another doubt in her life.

"Someone to share things with. Someone who won't run off to New York."

Since she couldn't imagine doing such a thing, Charlotte found it exceedingly easy to promise that. Would her reward for her acquiescence be a kiss? She closed her eyes and shook her head. She was becoming obsessed with his kisses.

Yet, as if he read her mind, he complied.

But this kiss was not a sweet seal to their engagement. It was fiery hot, passionate and exciting. He held her tightly as if there were no one else on the planet. And for a long time, Charlotte forgot that there was.

8

Sarah displayed no sign of surprise when Asher told her of his engagement the next morning. He realized he had expected some show of astonishment instead of the almost smug expression on her face.

Looking at her quizzically, he asked her to step into his office.

"Congratulations. I think it's about time," Sarah said as she closed the door behind her.

"About time? Addie hasn't even been dead two months. I'm rushing."

"Actually, I think it's time that you found someone to love and marry. You and Addie were too much alike. Of course I know you two married to build the company. Now it's time you had a wife for yourself. It isn't as if you and Addie even lived together over the last three years. Be happy, boss, and don't worry about timing."

Asher opened his mouth to clear up Sarah's misconception, then snapped it shut. If she wanted to think this was a love match, who was he to burst her bubble? At least Lottie knew the truth.

He frowned and moved to sit behind his desk. At least he thought she did. She'd mentioned love yesterday. But Asher knew love was some nebulous emotion that supposedly bound people together. A marriage could succeed well without it when the partners respected each other and had similar goals.

Anxious to get to work, he began to list the tasks he had for Sarah. Once he had the wedding behind him, he could concentrate on business. He dictated a short list of tasks such as get the license, find a childcare facility for daily drop offs since he and Lottie would be home evenings and weekends.

"And how does Charlotte feel about this?" Sarah asked when he paused.

"She agreed to marry me," he said.

A feeling of complacency filled him. She'd agreed. And he wouldn't let her change her mind.

"I don't mean about that, I mean about all your plans for the wedding. Usually the bride decides these things."

He frowned.

"I don't know."

"A word of advice, boss. At least ask. You should be making these plans together."

"Call her in," he ordered.

Charlotte entered Asher's office in response to Sarah's request. She looked first at Asher, then at Sarah. Was this some kind of meeting?

"Congratulations and best wishes," Sarah said, smiling warmly.

Charlotte smiled back, feeling nervous. The more she thought about this, the more nervous she grew. Yet knowing how she felt about Asher, she couldn't stand aside and let someone else marry him and share a life with him and the twins.

She wanted that for herself.

"I've asked Sarah to make arrangements for the ceremony. She'll reserve a room at City Hall on Friday and find out what we need to do for a license."

"Actually, Asher, we need to talk about this some more," Charlotte said as she sat in one of the chairs near the desk.

"What's there to talk about? You agreed to marry me, that's the end of it."

She shook her head.

"No, it's the beginning. But that's not what I mean. After I got home last night, I began to think. This is my only wedding. I don't want some hurried affair at City Hall."

He leaned back in amazement.

"You aren't going to tell me you want some full-blown wedding that takes six months or longer to plan?"

"No. It's not like I have a big family or anything. But I do have some good friends whom I'd want to attend. And I expect you have some friends who should be there and your grandfather. I want a church wedding. I thought maybe we could have the ceremony at a little chapel near Columbus Avenue. If Sarah wouldn't mind seeing if we could use it Friday, we could still meet your schedule. But I'm not getting married at City Hall."

"How many friends are you talking about?" he asked suspiciously.

"I want the members of my team to be invited. And I have several neighbors to ask. And my friend Susie can stand up with me. About ten in all."

"Ten."

He stared at her.

He hadn't expected this. A quick ceremony to make it legal was all he anticipated. It was what he and Addie had done.

Now Charlotte was talking like a real bride. Which, of course, she was. For a moment, Asher really looked at her.

He wondered if he'd done the right thing for Lottie in insisting she marry him. She was young, had her whole life ahead of her. Was it fair to tie her to a man who already had two children, who had one business marriage behind him?

Would she grow to resent him as the years rolled by?

The image of the twins arose. They had a new nanny today, Jennifer McConnall. Sarah had seen to that. But how long before she left?

The girls needed stability and love. Lottie would provide both. And he'd do anything to insure his daughters got the best.

"There're several people who would be quite upset if Asher had a wedding and didn't invite them," Sarah added.

"I don't need your input," he snapped.

"Sure you do," Charlotte said. "If she's the wedding coordinator, we both need to listen to her. So how many should we plan from Asher's side?" she asked Sarah.

"His senior management staff, his attorney and several friends from the various organizations he belongs to. Whomever he asks to be best man. Add his grandfather and we are probably talking at least a dozen or more."

"That'd be more than three dozen people at the ceremony," he said.

"He's always so good with numbers, isn't he?" Charlotte said proudly. "What's the matter with that? And don't forget the girls. They have to be there."

"They're babies. They don't belong at a wedding."

"Yes, they do. They have to be there."

Charlotte refused to get ruffled, though his dark look had her heart racing. She'd considered things long and hard last night. If she was to be coerced into a marriage of convenience—Asher's convenience—she insisted on having a say in things.

Start as you mean to go on, her foster mother had often said.

Asher stared at her for a long moment, then nodded.

"Do as the bride says, Sarah."

The week flew by. Charlotte agonized over her agreement to this marriage every moment. Was she doing the right thing?

Distracted by her thoughts, she was constantly teased into paying attention by her team members. Awed at first by her forthcoming marriage to the boss, everyone soon settled into a routine when they saw she made no changes in her demeanor.

Charlotte was not a person to put on airs. Besides, the entire situation seemed like some dream. How could she believe it, much less act on it?

When Asher suggested she move into the office near his, she declined. For the time being, she was a marketing analyst, and at work at least, she didn't want any favors for being the boss's wife.

"You're also part owner now, which makes you the boss," he said on Wednesday when she protested the move.

"After the wedding, and then only on paper. Compared to you and the other senior managers, I know so little. It will be years before I'll be ready to make major decisions. Maybe we should hold off on my getting shares."

"Hold off?" Asher stared at her in confusion. "The shares were what changed your mind. What do you mean, hold off? You're not trying to delay the wedding, are you?"

Exasperated, she shook her head.

"No, I'm not trying to delay anything—except putting shares in my name. I'd thought you'd be happy about that."

He narrowed his eyes. They were in his office to discuss how to present the World vision preliminary analysis in the best light. When he made a casual mention of her part ownership, Charlotte had to say something.

She felt a tremendous amount of guilt at the thought of taking the shares.

"I thought that was what tipped the scales so you said yes," he said thoughtfully.

She swallowed and looked at the notes on the sheet before her. She could hardly tell him she was marrying him to make sure no one else did. He'd want to know why, and that she couldn't tell him.

"I think we should wait, that's all."

"All right. You let me know when it's appropriate," he said.

In seconds, he was back into the World vision project.

By Friday morning, Charlotte was a nervous wreck. She'd packed enough clothes to cover any and all circumstances for the weekend. She'd have to come back and finish packing to move completely.

Arrangements had been made to have her furniture stored or disposed of. The apartment was on the market. She hoped someone wanted it right away.

During the week, she'd done her best to ignore the coming change in her life. But at the oddest times, she'd remember Asher's words in the meadow at his grandfather's.

This would be a real marriage.

Of course he'd want that. He planned to stay married for the rest of his life, and he was too virile to settle for some platonic relationship.

Then her thoughts would turn to the bed she'd seen in his apartment. Trying to imagine them together in it would cause a warm flush to invade her body.

Doubts would then spring up, and she'd wonder if she could go through with the wedding.

On Friday morning, as she was dressing, she still worried about whether she was doing the right thing.

"Charlotte, are you all right?" Susie asked.

Her friend was wearing a rose suit that suited her dark coloring.

Charlotte blinked. She was daydreaming again. She smiled at her friend and nodded.

"Yes, of course. A little nervous, I guess."

Her maid of honor touched her hair, the ends curled and resting on her shoulders.

"You look pretty. And this is so romantic. You never said a word about him before the last couple of weeks," Susie said.

"He was married before," Charlotte said dryly, hoping to deflect her friend's curiosity.

She'd bought a cream-colored suit for the ceremony at a

darling bridal shop in Union Street. The owner had insisted she needed a small hat with a veil. Studying herself in the mirror, Charlotte knew she looked pretty. The heightened color in her cheeks was not due to makeup, nor was the sparkle in her eyes. She was going to be married in a few hours.

"So the minute he's free, he sweeps you off your feet." Susie gave a huge sigh and laughed in glee.

"It's so romantic. I wish someone tall, dark and handsome would sweep me off my feet."

Charlotte started to correct Susie, then changed her mind. Let her friend continue to think it romantic. It'd only shatter her dreams if Charlotte told her the truth.

"I help, Daddy," Kennedy said as she knotted his shoelaces.

"Thank you, sweetheart. I think Daddy can tie his own shoes."

He lifted the shoe from her hands and struggled with the knot, wondering if it would be faster to just cut the thing and find a new pair of laces.

He heard a giggle from the bathroom.

"Madison, what are you doing?" he called.

He should have taken Sarah up on her offer to stop by earlier to get the girls. Or insisted the nanny come today. He had magnanimously given her the day off.

Now he was trying to get dressed with both twins underfoot. And both wanted to help.

He blamed Charlotte. She'd insisted they attend the wedding. Otherwise they could have stayed with Jennifer and known nothing about it.

"Noffing."

He might be new to parenting, but he was a fast study. Nothing always meant something. He dropped the shoe in the center of the bed to keep it out of Kennedy's hands and stormed into the bathroom.

Madison stood on the closed toilet seat, her face slathered in shaving cream. Her bright blue eyes peered out of white foam apprehensively. There was foam everywhere—on the walls, the mirror, her nightgown. Thank goodness he'd waited to dress them.

"Madison, I told you yesterday not to bother Daddy's things, didn't I?" he scolded.

"Wanna shave."

"Little girls don't need to shave. Even little boys don't need to shave."

Kennedy came to the door and laughed.

"Snowman," she said gleefully. "Me, too."

"No."

Asher steered Kennedy out of the bathroom and started to clean Madison.

He couldn't wait until Charlotte lived here. She could watch at least one of the girls. It had to be easier one-on-one.

At least he hoped so. He wasn't going through all this just to find out things hadn't improved.

Careful to keep the cream from his dress pants, he washed Madison's face and rinsed her hair. Then he sent her off to her room while he made an attempt to salvage the bathroom.

Tonight Lottie would be sharing this room. Would be sleeping in his bed.

He paused as he thought about that. He'd fantasized

about sleeping with her since that night in New York. When he'd mentioned he expected the marriage to be normal in every way, he'd halfway anticipated an objection. But she'd said nothing.

Tonight he could kiss her until they both were so hot and bothered they didn't know which way was up. Then he'd bring her to bed and make slow love all night long.

He had changed the sheets first thing after he got up this morning. His closet had been partially cleared to make room for her clothes.

He pushed some of the containers on the sink counter to the left. She could put her things beside them. It had been a long time since he'd shared with a woman.

"Daddy. Wanna see Lottie."

"I'll be there in a minute."

He hoped his daughters slept soundly tonight. Maybe he'd better take them to the park this afternoon to make sure they got plenty of exercise.

Vaguely excited about the day, Asher gave up analyzing why.

That was Lottie's job, he thought, smiling wryly. She loved to analyze things, didn't she?

He knew he'd made the right decision for his girls. Anything else was just a bonus.

Asher had sent a limo for Charlotte. She climbed into the back as if she'd been doing it all her life. The driver handed Susie in and then placed Charlotte's bags in the trunk.

"This is class. Are you always going to travel by limo?" Susie asked, examining everything.

"Of course not. Asher has a nice sedan. We drove to

Sonora in it last weekend."

"The little time we've had since your bombshell hasn't been enough. I want to know everything about this man. You're my best friend. I can't let you get married unless I approve," Susie teased.

"What do you want to know?" Charlotte asked, stalling for time.

"When did you realize you loved him?"

The answer came promptly.

"In a meadow in Sonora. Last weekend, just before he proposed."

"Oh, wow. Tell me more."

There was little to tell, Charlotte realized, but she did her best to make her brief courtship sound romantic and happy. She could be excused if she minimized how much time the twins were with them and exaggerated their time alone.

They'd never had a date, she realized. She'd be married and never get the chance to date Asher.

Ignoring the twinge of disappointment, she embellished every meeting, focusing on how he looked, what he said and how her heart melted whenever she looked at him.

Susie was positively glowing by the time the limo stopped at the small chapel. She hugged Charlotte.

"I wish you all the happiness in the world," she said as the driver opened the rear door.

Nervously, Charlotte walked beside her friend into the foyer. It was exactly eleven. The minister greeted her and they exchanged pleasantries.

Sarah stepped up, smiling broadly.

"You wouldn't be a bride without a bouquet."

She gave Charlotte a large bouquet of white and pale pink roses, baby's breath and trailing cream-colored ribbons that exactly matched her suit. A smaller bouquet was given to Susie.

Touched by Sarah's thoughtfulness, Charlotte hugged the older woman.

"Thank you."

Tears stung her eyes. Blinking rapidly, she tried to recapture her composure.

"Ready?" Sarah asked.

When Charlotte nodded, Sarah smiled.

"One more thing. Asher asked if I'd hold your glasses."

"My glasses? I need them."

"Humor the man, honey. He isn't asking for a lot."

Nodding, Charlotte slipped them off and handed them to Sarah. Everything in the distance blurred.

"When the organist begins to play the wedding march, you two start up the aisle," the minister said. "Your groom is already there. The music will begin as soon as I'm in place."

Charlotte nodded again, too choked up to speak. This was her wedding. It'd start in only seconds, and she would bind her life to Asher's for all time.

Susie smiled at her and moved to the door, listening for the musical cue. When it came, she opened the door wide.

Startled at all the people, Charlotte hesitated. She knew there couldn't be more than the three dozen or so people they'd discussed, but it seemed like a huge crowd. Every eye was on her. She froze.

"Come on, that's the wedding march," Susie whispered, nudging her.

At the front of the chapel, she saw Asher. He looked so tall and distant. While she couldn't see him clearly, she knew exactly what he looked like. His dark suit emphasized his dark hair, his tanned skin. She could feel the strength of his gaze from where she stood. Her gaze moved right. He'd asked his grandfather to be best man. She knew Silas must be happy.

Taking a breath, she stepped forward and almost tripped as she spotted two identical little girls peer around their daddy's legs and grin at her. Their dresses were pink, the exact color of the blossoms in her bouquet. Both looked adorable.

If nothing else, to be given a chance to raise these children made everything right.

Her heart melted and tears filled her eyes as she started up the aisle behind Susie.

When she reached Asher, he nodded and turned to face the minister.

"Hi, Lottie," Madison said.

"Hi, yourself," she whispered, smiling at the little girl.

"Dearly beloved," the minister began.

"Up!" Kennedy said, standing in front of Charlotte, holding her arms high.

"Me, too," Madison said.

"Not now," Asher said quietly.

"They could see better if they were up," Charlotte whispered.

She handed Susie her bouquet and reached to lift Kennedy. Settling her dress over her arm, she smiled brightly at Asher and faced the minister.

"And you talk about me spoiling them," he murmured.

Two seconds later, Asher had Madison in his arms, his expression impassive as if every groom held a toddler in his arms while exchanging vows with his bride.

The minister smiled broadly and began again.

Charlotte's eyes met Asher's. They faced each other as the age-old words were read. When Asher was asked if he'd take Charlotte as his wife, his voice rang out loud and true as he said, "I will."

The girls were quiet, impressed with the solemnity of the ceremony. When the minister asked Charlotte to repeat her vows, her grip tightened on Kennedy. She was not only marrying Asher Callahan, she was agreeing to become the mother of these two little girls. It was fitting that they participate in the ceremony.

It was awkward exchanging rings with an armful of little girl, but it was done.

"You may kiss your bride."

Light flared in Asher's eyes. Slowly he leaned closer until his lips brushed against Charlotte's.

"Daddy kiss Lottie," Madison announced.

"Me, too." Kennedy gave Charlotte a big smack on her cheek. Madison couldn't be outdone and demanded her father lean over again so she could kiss Lottie.

"I feel very married now," Charlotte said softly, her heart in her throat.

Susie patted her friend's arm.

"Congratulations!" she said. "I have my phone for pictures. Walk down the aisle and greet whomever you have to, then come back for pictures."

Things happened in a blur. Charlotte met a half a dozen people, and hoped she could remember their names. She was glad for the familiar faces of the men and women she worked with and her neighbors, happy they came to share her special day.

Silas looked like an old friend. He hugged her tightly.

"Be good to my boy," he said gruffly.

She nodded and blinked. If she got through the day without her emotions tangling up so much they spilled out, she'd be extremely lucky.

Sarah had arranged a small luncheon reception at a private club in North Beach. She handed maps to the guests and shooed them on their way.

"The bridal couple needs to have their pictures taken. They'll join us soon."

She made sure Asher knew where the place was, then hurried away.

Susie enlisted the help of Mark from Charlotte's project team to take pictures so Susie could also be in some. She staged every pose, some with Asher and Charlotte alone, others with the twins, the minister and then with herself and Silas. Finally she was satisfied they'd done enough.

"We'll take more at the reception," she said as they hurried out.

Charlotte sipped champagne and smiled. She nibbled the buffet luncheon and smiled. Thanking each guest for coming, she smiled. By mid afternoon her cheeks hurt, her feet were beginning to ache and she felt light-headed. But she didn't want the day to end. She was having a wonderful time.

And when they left, it'd be to return to Asher's apartment, to begin their new life together.

Several times during the afternoon she caught sight of her wedding ring—a plain gold band, which shone in the light. It felt strange on her finger—and right. Once she looked from it to Asher and found his gaze on her. Heat pumped through her, and she visualized his big bed. Swallowing, she turned away and tried desperately to remember what the conversation was about.

Every time she thought about making this marriage real, normal, as Asher had said, her heart started to pound and her thoughts became so tangled she hadn't a clue how to think straight. It was Friday. They'd go home after their reception, put the children to bed and begin their life together.

In his bed.

Neither had to be to work before Monday. Which meant they had two entire days to do nothing but—

"You look flushed. Too warm in here?" Sarah asked.

"No, I'm fine. It's a wonderful reception. I can't believe you put everything together so fast, on such short notice. Everything's so lovely. Of course I know how efficient you are. Asher couldn't manage without you. But this is really above and beyond—"

Charlotte stopped abruptly. She was babbling. Sneaking another peek at Asher, she was pleased to see him talking with one of his friends. That gave her the opportunity to study him without his knowing it.

He looked as calm as he did in staff meetings. And why not? As far as he was concerned, this was merely another deal. A bargain made and carried out. He probably hadn't given tonight a second thought.

But it was all Charlotte could think about. She remembered how warm his fingers had felt against her skin when he tucked back her hair or clasped his hands with hers as they walked together in Columbia. Tonight he'd touch her all over with those same fingers, those masculine hands. Kiss her until she couldn't remember her name.

Suddenly she wished with all her heart that this was truly a normal marriage. That he loved her as much as she loved him.

How would she stand it year after year—to want his devotion and receive only courtesy?

He looked up and caught her eye. Smiling, he gestured for her to join him. When she did so, he encircled her shoulders and drew her close.

"Are you about ready to leave?"

"Now?"

Panic gripped her.

"We've eaten, spoken to everyone, even cut the cake. Two or three people keep looking at their watches, and I suspect they don't want to be the first to leave. Grandpa needs to get started to get home before dinnertime. Any reason to stay?"

She shook her head. "I guess not. Where are the girls?"

"Grandpa has Kennedy. I think Sarah took charge of Madison a while ago."

"Give the woman a raise. She deserves it."

"For taking one of the twins or for today?"

"Both."

Bravely Charlotte tilted her head and looked directly into Asher's eyes.

"I think it was a lovely reception. The ceremony was beautifully done."

"Even with two squirming girls in arms?"

"They didn't squirm, they were very well behaved."

"No disappointments?" he asked.

"Why would I? The day's been perfect. Susie was

enthralled with the limo."

"And you?"

She nodded.

"Thank you, Asher. It's been perfect."

"And not over yet."

Heat licked every cell in her body.

"No, I guess not," she said faintly.

Far too soon, they bade farewell to their guests, gathered their little girls and got into the limousine. Settling in the soft leather seat, Charlotte tried to act normal.

"Lottie tell story," Madison said from the car seat opposite where Asher had placed her.

"Mommy now," Asher said.

"Mommy gone," Kennedy said.

"Lottie is your mommy now. You can call her mommy," Asher explained.

"Mommy?" Madison looked around.

"Asher, I think you're confusing them. They can continue to call me Lottie."

"Then it will get confusing when we have kids of our own. Madison, Kennedy, Lottie is your new mommy. Your first mommy is gone, but Lottie will be your new mommy. Mommy two."

"Mommy two?" Madison tried to understand.

Charlotte couldn't say a word. Her body hummed from his casual comment about their own children.

"Lottie Mommy two?" Kennedy said.

"Yes, Lottie is Mommy two."

9

The limousine driver carried Charlotte's bags to the apartment. Asher took Kennedy and Charlotte held Madison's hand as they rode in silence in the elevator. The girls released their hold and ran to the door when they reached the apartment. Asher tipped the driver, unlocked the door and let the girls dash in.

"Go to your room and I'll be there in a minute so you can change," he instructed them.

He carried Charlotte's bags inside, then turned to look at her.

"Coming?"

Silently, she nodded then reluctantly stepped inside.

So much for her dream of her husband carrying her over the threshold of her new home. Closing the door, she tried to act sensibly. This wasn't a love relationship. She knew with certainty that Asher had never thought about it.

He carried her luggage to his bedroom. She took off her wispy hat and set it on the table near the door, then headed to the twins' bedroom. Their dresses were so darling, she didn't want to waste a moment getting them off lest they ruin them.

Did every bride feel a bit let down when the festivities ended and real life returned?

"I'll help the girls change," she called.

She was struggling to snap Madison's jeans when Asher appeared in the doorway.

"I can finish up, if you want to change."

He'd already done so. The casual slacks and pullover shirt looked comfortable. But for a moment, Charlotte missed the dark suit. He'd looked breathtakingly handsome today.

"Okay. What did you want to do now? What should I wear?"

"I thought we'd take these two to the park and let them run. They had enough sugar at the reception to make them higher than a kite."

"I won't be long."

"Take time to unpack if you like. We can go ahead and you can find us when you're done," he suggested. "Remember, I've seen how these girls help in packing. I doubt their unpacking technique is much better."

Charlotte murmured agreement and headed for the bedroom. She wasn't precisely sure what she expected, but it wasn't this. She thought there should be something to extend their special day.

Maybe a suggestion for a candlelight dinner. He could have taken her to that place he'd mentioned before, where there was dancing. That would have been nice.

She changed into comfortable jeans and a pink top. Exploring his room, Charlotte discovered he'd made space for her clothes in his closet and left two drawers of the dresser ajar to show they were empty. Hearing the twins and Asher leave, she began to put away her clothes. She fingered his business suits hanging in the large closet and remembered Asher wearing each of them. His scent filled the space so much she almost felt as if he were there.

Lovingly, she hung the cream suit she'd bought especially for today and wondered when, if ever, she'd wear it again. She hung her other suits, then closed the door. The suitcases she stacked near the front door. She remembered Asher mentioned a storage space in the garage area. The cases could be put there later.

Wandering through the apartment, Charlotte tried to impress upon herself that it was her new home. It seemed alien. None of her things were here yet. The master bedroom and bath were on one side of the living area with the twins' room, the guest room and the second bath on the other side.

She peeked into the extra room. Asher's first nanny had left the place immaculate. Had that situation worked, would he have sought Charlotte for marriage?

Probably not, she mused. Shaking off her vague sense of disappointment, she headed for the park.

It was easy to locate her family from the twins' shrieks of laughter. There was a small playground area with swings, climbing apparatus and tall slides. Asher was pushing the girls in the swings. Not high, but to little girls it probably seemed daring. They laughed and shouted to go higher and higher.

"Need help?" Charlotte asked, joining them.

"Want to swing?" he asked, grinning at her.

The slight breeze from the bay had tousled his hair, giving him a rakish air. Gradually Charlotte relaxed. She smiled. This would work.

"No, I'll just watch."

"Go slide," Kennedy said.

"Whoops."

Asher caught her and stopped the swing.

"She doesn't seem to understand about not letting go before the swing stops."

"I'll take her to the slide. You can keep pushing Madison," Charlotte said.

He looked at her, his gaze trailing from the top of her glossy black hair and down the length of her. Leaning over, he brushed his lips against hers.

"You look pretty, sweetheart."

Charlotte's legs almost gave way. His compliment was the last thing she expected.

"Thank you," she murmured, more flustered than she should be.

She'd never expected Asher to say anything like that. She watched him while she kept an eye on Kennedy. He looked younger laughing with his daughter. She was used to the serious businessman.

To see him in a different light felt odd. And intimate. None of the other employees at Callahan Associates had seen this side of him. Not even, she suspected, Addie.

Charlotte was as tired as the twins when they headed for home. During the afternoon they'd run, played tag and red light green light and tried every piece of playground equipment.

"A quick dinner and they'll be ready for bed," she murmured as they reached the apartment.

She wasn't sure she wouldn't be, also. It had been a long day. And every moment, she'd thought about being in Asher's bed that night. And that they were married.

"I should have asked what you wanted to do about

dinner," Asher said as they walked into the kitchen together. "We can find a café if you don't want to cook tonight."

For a moment, Charlotte felt like an old married woman. The ease with which they spent the afternoon proved they were compatible.

But the thrumming of her heart had her tied up in knots. She wondered if, after years of living together, she'd eventually grow used to being with Asher.

"The girls are too tired to go out, don't you think?" she asked as she peered into the refrigerator. It seemed well stocked. "They'd be cranky while we waited for the food at a restaurant. There must be something we can fix that's fast."

Besides, it was her wedding night. If she couldn't go dancing with her new husband, she surely didn't want to be responsible for the twins when they were so tired.

"What do they like to eat?"

"Everything. And lots of it."

Charlotte smiled.

"They're probably getting ready to grow again. I remember my foster mother always saying when kids eat like there's no tomorrow, it meant time for new clothes and shoes soon."

She stopped talking.

"Do you keep in touch with your foster parents?" Asher asked, leaning casually against the wall near the sink, watching her.

She shook her head and withdrew some ground beef from the refrigerator.

"Do you have the rest of the ingredients for spaghetti?"

"In the cupboard. Why not?"

She looked up, surprised he'd even ask.

"We weren't close. They saw me as a glorified baby-sitter. I represented whatever the state was paying that month for my care. I never really thought of them as parents—just people watching me until I was old enough to do it myself."

She shrugged, trying to make sure none of the hurt showed. She'd so longed for love and acceptance.

Suddenly a thought struck her.

Whirling to face him, she said, "You don't think Kennedy and Madison will feel that way about me, do you?"

Slowly Asher unfolded his arms and straightened. He took the three steps necessary to reach her and shook his head.

"They love you already. And you love them. It shows, Lottie. You'll be the only mother they'll ever know or remember. They'll love you always."

He took the meat from her hands and put it on the counter. Threading his fingers through her shiny hair, he tilted her head until she faced him.

"Thank you for becoming their mother."

His gaze touched every inch of her face.

"The sun kissed your cheeks. They're pink. And your black hair looks like it has light shining through it. There are sparkles in your eyes that remind me of starlight. And your mouth has tempted me all day."

He captured that tempting mouth with his.

Charlotte reached out and drew his body close to hers until she was nestled against his hard length. She felt as if she were flying. Breathless with delight, she wished the moment could continue forever.

Daringly she began to respond, to kiss him back, opening

her lips to his quest, letting her tongue dance with his. She hoped he was as excited about kissing her as she was about him holding her. She'd die if she couldn't bring him the same pleasure.

Asher released her mouth to trail kisses along her jaw. His fingers tipped her head back and he rained kisses along her throat. His tongue licked, his lips tantalized. The minutes ticked by until Charlotte could think of nothing but Asher and the delight she found in his arms. Her blood was boiling, her breathing almost nonexistent. Whirling sensations crested and splashed. Could one person contain such happiness?

She opened her eyes to find his staring into hers. Her love for him was so strong she thought she'd burst.

"We'd better get something for those two or we'll have raving maniacs tormenting us to death in about ten minutes," he said.

She came back to earth with a crash.

Preparing dinner, Charlotte felt as if she existed in some kind of time warp. She was reminded of her first night in New York after being coerced into traveling there with Asher. Hadn't he practically coerced her into this marriage?

That wasn't fair. She'd gone into it with her eyes wide open.

After the girls ate, Charlotte went to run their bath while they helped Asher clean up. Once they were ready for bed, all of them gathered together to read a story. It didn't take the twins long to fall asleep.

Charlotte delayed leaving the girls' room as long as possible. Her heart raced in her chest, and she found it difficult to focus on anything. The minutes passed and each one brought her that much closer to bedtime. And Asher's large bed.

Wondering if Asher was as anxious as she was, she at last turned and headed for the living room. She wondered no more. He sat in one of the easy chairs, reading reports from work.

This was their wedding night and he was working.

But of course to him the day had meant nothing beyond a convenient new mother for the sake of his daughters. She cleared her throat.

Looking up, he put the papers on his lap and gestured to the sofa.

"What are we doing with the girls on Monday?" Charlotte asked as she sat down.

"I believe Jennifer is still planning to be here."

"I thought Sarah was looking into day care for them, where there are other little children. It'd be good for them to interact with others their age. Another advantage would be that we wouldn't be dependent on a single person who could get sick or choose not to come for some other reason."

"Jennifer seems reliable. And if she can't make it one day, you or I could stay home with them. There's been enough disruption in their lives. I'd rather not introduce day care just yet."

Charlotte nodded and looked out the window. Asher made sense. There had been a lot of disruption in their lives over the last few weeks.

And in her own, as well.

"I almost forgot."

Asher reached into the briefcase beside his chair and

withdrew a large envelope. He tossed it to Charlotte.

"What is this?" she asked, slipping her finger beneath the flap.

She withdrew the legal documents and saw shares of Callahan Associates in her name.

"I thought we were going to wait," she said slowly.

"I keep my bargains, Lottie. That was part of the deal. Why wait?" he asked.

Part of the deal.

Had she let herself confuse his earlier kiss with genuine caring? Slowly, feeling drained and tired, Charlotte rose. She tucked the stock certificates in the envelope and turned toward the hallway.

"I'm tired. I'm going to bed."

But not in his bed.

There were limits—and Charlotte had reached hers.

No pretending that this was a love match. No more expecting that life would have a happy ending. She'd agreed to this marriage and would live up to her end—acting as a mother to Madison and Kennedy. But she'd continue to work hard and make a life for herself apart from watching children.

"I'll be along in a few minutes," Asher said.

She gathered her nightie and used the twins' bathroom to brush her teeth. She slipped into the guest room and didn't bother with a light. She pulled back the covers, thankful to see it freshly made up, and climbed in. Huddling beneath the light blanket, she turned her back to the door and tried to sleep.

Images of the day danced behind her eyelids—Susie's excitement, the twins peering around their father's legs, the reception, the afternoon at the park. She'd never spent much time daydreaming about a wedding day, so she couldn't be disappointed.

It had been a nice ceremony, with all the proper touches, including Asher's kiss.

But the kiss before dinner was the one she remembered.

The overhead light flashed on.

"What are you doing in here?" Asher's voice spoke from the doorway. "I had to look over the entire apartment for you."

She rolled on her back, narrowed her eyes against the sudden light and looked at him.

"I said I was going to sleep. I'm tired."

"This isn't my bed."

"No, but it's mine," she returned, sitting up to face him.

If they were going to have this out now, she wanted to be in a better position. Maybe she should stand. No, her nightgown was too filmy for that.

"What are you talking about? You know I expected this marriage to be normal in every way. Including sleeping together. We talked about it."

"No, Asher, you dictated what you wanted. I hardly know you. You don't know me. I understand what you want, and after we get to know each other—"

"What better way to know each other than to sleep together?"

"Not tonight."

He hesitated, his eyes boring into hers.

"When, then?"

His voice sounded calm, but Charlotte detected the hint of frustration.

"When we know each other better," she said bravely.

Her heart pounded as she surreptitiously wiped damp palms against the blanket.

"We married. I'm the mommy of your girls. I'll fulfill my part of this marriage deal."

"But not tonight?"

She shook her head. "I'm not saying no, just not yet."

Asher stared at her for another moment, then spun around, left and wanted to slam the door behind him in his frustration. But he stopped. That would likely wake the twins and he didn't need them up now. Slowly he shut the door.

He walked down the hall to his bedroom. Again he quietly closed the door though every inclination was to slam it to dissipate some of the letdown that roiled inside.

He'd expected to find Lottie waiting in his bed a few moments ago. Thinking he was being courteous, he'd let her use the bathroom first. Get ready first. When he'd come into the room, it was as empty as he'd left it on the way to their wedding.

Blast it, what was she doing? He'd made it perfectly clear that he wanted a normal marriage. Had she married him for the shares of stock? Now that she had that, she didn't feel compelled to do more?

He should have held off on giving them to her.

Yet hadn't she suggested that very thing? Maybe it wasn't the stock.

Was she shy, he wondered.

Not if her kiss in the kitchen earlier had been anything to go by. He could still feel her hands on his back, tracing his muscles, clutching him tightly against his sweet little body.

Slowly the frustration drained away. He'd expected something different on this night. But if she didn't wish to share his bed willingly, he didn't want her there. He wanted a wife, someone to share his life with, not a martyr.

And she had a point. They really didn't know each other that well.

Asher headed for the bathroom. He'd take a cold shower and see if he could fall asleep. And in the morning, he'd try to come up with a way to convince Lottie they belonged together in every way.

The next morning, when Asher entered the kitchen, Charlotte greeted him with a bright smile and a distant, reserved manner.

The girls were already dressed and making inroads into cinnamon toast. Their juice had been poured, and from the orange mustaches on matching faces, already sampled.

Asher watched Charlotte as she bustled around.

He wanted her. She was beautiful. Sweet inside and out. He loved watching her work when calculating returns on investments, or bathing his daughters, or cooking a meal.

He also appreciated her wariness. She was right. They didn't know each other that well. They hadn't even had a date. It'd been go, go, go from the moment he returned from Thailand.

She was his wife and she hadn't even given him a good-morning kiss.

He tried to ignore that fact.

"Want eggs or something?" she asked.

"What are you having?"

He pulled out a chair and sat, fascinated by her. The jeans

fit her bottom snugly, outlining her curves and shapely legs. Her loose T-shirt draped her torso, drifting over the soft shape of her breasts. She'd left her hair down and her glasses off. Color stained her cheeks. He felt a kick of desire.

With a glance at the twins, Asher knew there was no way to get Charlotte alone right now much as he wanted to. He'd had more trouble than he expected falling asleep last night. Soon, he hoped things would be different.

"I already ate. I woke up early."

She avoided looking at him.

"But I can fix you anything."

"I'll have cinnamon toast like the girls," he said. "And coffee."

She nodded and placed a steaming mug before him.

"I had the coffee ready," she said with a polite smile.

He caught her wrist before she could draw away and looked up, meeting her eyes. Color rose in her cheeks. Asher took that as a sign that she wasn't indifferent. Or was he clutching at straws?

Slowly he tugged gently, pulling her down for a kiss.

She tasted sweet and cinnamony. Conscious of the twins avidly watching, he kept the brush of lips light. But it only whetted his appetite for his wife. He wanted more than a light kiss first thing in the morning.

"I thought we might go to the zoo today," Asher said as he watched Lottie prepare his toast.

"Take the girls. I have to go home."

The unexpected reply hit him hard.

"What do you mean?"

"I wanted to use this weekend to finish packing

everything. I have a moving company coming on Monday to take my furniture to storage. But there are things I want to bring here."

Asher didn't realize how tense he'd been until he felt his muscles relax. She wasn't leaving, merely going to get her things. After the weekend, this apartment would be her home.

"We can help, if you like."

She smiled at the twins.

"I don't think so. I can manage fine by myself. You take the girls."

Lottie was driving him crazy, Asher thought on Thursday morning as he tilted back in his chair in his office and gazed at the San Francisco Bay. From the whitecaps that dotted the expanse, he knew it was windy. But the sun shone and the air was crystal clear. He wished his life was as pristine as the view.

He still slept alone. Every night she'd come up with some excuse and reiterated the one that they didn't know each other well enough. But how she expected them to get to know each other better was a mystery to him.

She'd spent the entire weekend packing.

Monday night she'd gone to clean the apartment so she could get the security deposit back. He'd given her twenty percent of Callahan Associates and she wanted her security deposit returned.

Tuesday he'd been tied up dealing with the situation in Bangkok. By the time he'd reached home, she'd been asleep.

Last night, she'd brought work home and stayed up long after he headed for bed.

Every day she remained friendly, but the wall between them seemed to grow thicker. What happened to his expectations of a wife so grateful for the Callahan stock she'd be more than willing to fall in with his plans?

He sipped his coffee and shook his head.

Lottie wasn't any more likely to fall in with anyone's plans than he was. She had definite ideas of how things should be.

Was that part of the problem? Had their marriage not measured up in some way?

But how could that be? It was a business arrangement first, last and always. What was there not to measure up? She received her shares of the stock, he obtained a mother for his kids.

"And what did I get out of it?" he asked aloud. "I want a wife."

His marriage to Addie had been a business relationship for the most part. But even with that as the premise for their marriage, they'd found pleasure sleeping together.

Tonight he'd get the twins to bed early and see what he could find out how Lottie viewed their future.

Anticipation began to simmer as he looked forward to the evening.

Charlotte arrived home minutes before Asher. He'd suggested they drive together, but after Tuesday, when he'd been so late coming home, she outright refused.

She didn't want to be stuck at work if he ran late, and it was likely there'd be occasions when she'd be late and didn't want to hold him up. One of the two of them had to get home each day when the nanny was due to leave.

She spoke with Jennifer for a few minutes, then hugged

the twins and invited them to come with her while she changed. They talked excitedly about their day. Jennifer had taken them to the park and they told Charlotte about seeing a dog. *Was it the first one they'd seen?* she wondered.

Charlotte had just slipped off her blouse and skirt when Asher appeared in the door. The sound of the children talking had masked his arrival. He held his suit jacket over his shoulder by one finger. Raising an eyebrow, he let his gaze scan her scantily clad figure, a slow, sexy smile holding her enthralled.

Charlotte gathered her casual clothes and fled to the bathroom. Closing the door behind her, she heard the girls greet their father.

Blood pounding through her veins, she leaned against the wall and tried to analyze the feelings that coursed through her. His gaze had felt like a touch. She was agonizingly aware of each inch of bare skin glowing with heat. She dressed, then delayed leaving the safety the bathroom afforded. How long could she stall?

The knock on the door answered her silent question.

She opened it and gazed at Asher.

He smiled and leaned over to kiss her gently.

Involuntarily her eyes shifted to the big bed. The girls were bouncing on it. It still looked huge. She'd never even sat on the side.

He kissed her again, then gently moved her outside the bathroom and closed the door in her face.

Dinner seemed to fly by. Charlotte tried to delay its finish, but that proved impossible with the twins anxious to play for a short while before bath and bed. Even the dishes were finished in record time.

Asher's constant gaze about drove her crazy. He watched her through dinner as if she'd disappear if he didn't. He leaned against the counter while she did the dishes, discussing various projects at the company, asking for her input.

He helped with the children's bathing, and the four of them sat on the sofa for reading time. But tonight, Charlotte's voice wouldn't work. She insisted Asher read to the children.

The sound of his voice affected her nervous system as strongly as did his touch. She closed her eyes and listened to his rich tones bring the story alive for his daughters. All too soon he finished. It was time to put the children to bed.

Charlotte wanted to crawl into bed with Madison, pull the baby's blanket over her head and hide away. But Asher was right there with her, and when the last kiss had been given, his hand reached for hers.

"Come with me."

Charlotte's heart pounded. Now what?

He returned to the living room and sat on the sofa. She sat beside him and turned so she could face him.

"We talked about a real marriage," he began.

She nodded, heat flooding her. "I want that, too. But really, we hardly know each other and it's not easy for me to just jump into bed with someone."

He nodded. "I know. It's not no, it's not yet."

She tried to smile. He'd remembered.

"So how do you propose we get to know each other until we are comfortable together?" he asked.

She dropped her gaze. Thinking about it, she realized she really didn't have a instant way to get to know him better and have him know her better without the danger of giving away her feelings.

He still held her hand. Gently his thumb rubbed across the back.

"Maybe dating? Isn't that what most couples do?" he suggested. "We could go out just the two of us. It'd be better than taking the girls so we can focus on us."

She nodded. Would he come to like her if he knew her better? Come to care for her?

10

"Daddy, want water."

Madison ran into the living room.

"Madison, honey, you should be in bed," Asher said, rising.

"I'm firstee."

"Okay, just a little water."

"Me, too." Kennedy came up the hall, dragging her blanket. "Me, too."

"I guessed as much," Asher said dryly.

Charlotte rose beside him.

"Come on, baby girls, we'll get some nice cold water and then tuck you up in bed again."

"I wanna story," Madison said when Asher picked her up and carried her into the kitchen.

"We already had our story for tonight," Asher said.

Charlotte brought both girls small glasses of water. She watched them drink without lifting her gaze to Asher.

He watched her, wondering if she thought by ignoring him she could change anything. Frustration touched him. He thought they'd make some headway, until the girls interrupted. It was enough to drive a man crazy.

"This time stay in your bed," Asher said as he scooped up one twin. He looked at Charlotte. "Coming?"

She shook her head. "You can tuck them in without me."

He hesitated, wondering if she planned to bolt while he was busy with the girls. Deciding not to press the issue, he shrugged and held out a hand for his other daughter. "I'll tuck you in, and this time you go straight to sleep, all right?" he said as they walked down the hall.

Once they were settled, Asher headed for the living room and saw Lottie sitting in a chair. He paused in the archway. She looked like she meant to stay there for quite some time. She met his gaze and never looked away, but by the determined tilt to her chin Asher wasn't sure she was ready to take up where they left off on the sofa.

"I want to talk to you," she said and pointed to another chair. "Please."

He crossed the room and sat where she indicated. What he wanted to do was pull her from the chair and kiss her until neither knew their own names.

But she seemed firmly ensconced in the chair and didn't look as if she'd be pleased.

"About?" he asked, hiding his frustration with difficulty.

"What you were saying earlier. About our marriage. Different things."

She swallowed hard. Try as she might to hide it, Asher could spot her nervousness from his seat. Slowly he leaned back, curious what she might have to say. For a moment his business sense took over.

How would she be at negotiations? Addie had been a natural, but Charlotte seemed too soft, too nice.

"So talk."

She cleared her throat.

"I was going to wait for Saturday. I thought it might be better, but now I guess I have to tell you tonight."

Uncertainty hit Asher. He focused on Lottie, forgetting instantly about work, negotiating skills and his first wife.

"Tell me what?"

She cleared her throat again.

"I'm returning the shares of Callahan Associates. I have thought about it all week and truly I don't want them."

"Why not? I thought that was what you did want, part ownership in a business. You said so."

Nodding, she agreed.

"But not handed to me. I don't feel I've earned the shares. And that's what I really want—to feel I've earned my way. To be paid because I agreed to become your wife is cheating us both. I don't want them, Asher."

He listened, stunned. Did she mean to end the marriage as well as the partnership? Suddenly he knew he couldn't take that. He had to make her see they couldn't end their marriage. The girls would be devastated.

He suspected he'd be devastated.

"So what do you want?"

"Actually, I want to look for a new job," she said.

"What? What are you talking about? You can't leave the company."

The news shocked him. He rose and strode to the window and gazed out, not seeing anything. How could she even suggest leaving? Was that the first step?

"I can't stay. I'll never know if I'm getting anywhere because my ideas are solid and my experience is growing or because I'm the boss's wife."

Slowly Asher turned to look at her. She wanted to leave because she was the boss's wife? He knew how important doing well in business meant to her. But he couldn't shake the fear that this was but the first step.

"You're not ending our marriage," he said.

Her eyes widened in surprise.

Shaking her head, she said, "No. I thought we agreed this is forever. I should be the girls' mother."

"And my wife."

"Well, yes, that, too." She cleared her throat a third time. "Actually I wanted to talk to you about that, as well. Oh, not that I want to end the marriage. We only got married a week ago."

"Some might say the marriage is still pending consummation," Asher remarked dryly.

"I know, and that's the other thing we need to talk about."

"Tonight," he said firmly.

"Will you let me finish? This entire business has been rushed. I was convenient and had the child-care experience you needed—"

"Charlotte, just say whatever it is you want to say and let's go to bed."

"That's it, Asher. I'm not ready to go to bed with you. I know men can just hop into bed with whomever, but I can't."

"With whomever?" He took a step closer to her. "What do you think I am, some kind of stud who pounces on women whenever I get in the mood? I was married for six years to a business partner. We rarely shared a bed and that suited both of us. But we kept our vows and didn't seek entertainment elsewhere. Then she left, and for the last three of those years

I've been alone."

"That's just it. You've been alone and now you're not and you want me."

"You got that right. I do want you."

"You know as well as I do that there is no reciprocal love in this relationship. What you started to say earlier about dating and all. I think we need more time to get to know each other and develop some kind of friendship before we start sleeping together. So yes, I'd be up to dating," she said in a rush.

Her words made sense, but the timing was off. She should have said something last week. He couldn't wait for them to become friends. He wanted her more and more each day. The wall she'd built between them since last Friday had grown, not diminished. If he left her to her own devices, would he ever breach it?

He stepped near and held out his hand.

"Come with me for a minute. Just a minute."

She hesitated, then took his hand. She stood so close he could smell the faint scent of roses she always wore. It teased his senses and made him more aware of her than ever. She was petite, just reaching his shoulder. Her figure was dainty and feminine and drew him like a magnet drew iron. But he had an idea she hadn't a clue how he felt.

He walked with her into the bedroom, ignoring the bed and moving to stand before the full-length mirror near the closet. He pulled her in front of him and looked at her in the mirror.

"Look at yourself and tell me you don't understand why I want you. Only you. Your hair is beautiful, shiny and thick and soft as a baby's."

Slowly his fingers threaded in the wavy strands, reveling in the silky feel. He didn't know how she kept it so pretty, but it was. He pulled it from her face, letting the tresses slip over and through his fingers, relishing the sensations. His eyes met hers.

"Your skin resembles peaches and cream. You're so young you don't have a single wrinkle yet, and the texture is as pure as the finest porcelain."

His index finger lightly grazed her cheek. Instantly her color deepened, and Asher felt the pull of attraction grow stronger.

"I love it when you blush. Most women these days are incapable, but the slightest thing sets you off."

She closed her eyes with a groan.

He leaned forward to whisper in her ear, "Shyness in this liberal society is uncommon and all the more precious for being so."

Opening her eyes a slit, she looked at the reflection of the two of them.

Asher kept his face beside hers, his mouth inches from her ear. Resting his hands on her shoulders, he let his gaze blatantly follow the shapely contours of her body.

"You are feminine and sexy, Lottie. I've wanted you since that first night in New York. The first time you slipped off your glasses, I was gone. Your eyes are dark and mysterious and drive me wild. Sometimes you look at me as if you know something I don't know. Other times you look at me as if I'm someone special, still other times like I'm the biggest idiot on the face of the earth. I love the special times best."

Tears flooded those eyes, and Asher hesitated.

But when she smiled, he continued.

"When I look at you, I see the future, our future. We may never have that reciprocal love you spoke of, Lottie, but we can have a strong bond. I want to spend my life with you, and making love with you will be a part of it. But not because you are merely some woman who happens to be passing by. It's only because you are who you are. Sexy, enticing, enthralling."

"Asher, no one has ever said one of those things about me. Are you trying some masterful selling technique here?" she murmured, leaning against him, her hands coming to cover his on her shoulders.

Slowly he slid his palms across the front of her, passing her breasts till they rested on her waist. He didn't miss her shiver.

"I'm good at selling things. I hope I'm selling you on why I want you in my life. If you want to become friends first, I can wait. But it's going to be hard. And I want you to know how hard, just like I'll know it every day until you say yes."

Charlotte felt awed he'd given her so much power. Studying their figures in the mirror, she knew she'd love him until she died. No one had ever said such wonderful things about her.

She longed for Asher, for his kisses, for the touch of his hands. Should she keep denying what they both wanted? How important was love, anyway? Didn't she have enough for both of them? She'd married him knowing there was none on his part. Nothing had changed. She could explore the reaches of passion with this man. He'd take care of her. Just as he planned to take care of his daughters.

"I love you, Asher," she said softly.

He jerked and his eyes widened. Slowly he smiled.

"If that's what I get for pointing out your good features, I should have mentioned them earlier."

"I've loved you since before tonight," she said softly, her gaze holding his in the mirror.

He turned her in his arms and gazed directly at her.

"Lottie, I—"

She covered his mouth with her fingertips.

"No, don't say anything. We married for our own reasons. I have changed my mind about ownership in Callahan Associates, but not anything else. I thought I needed some more time to be your wife, but I don't. Not after this."

Moving her hand to the back of his head, she pulled him down for a kiss, as hot and wild as she could make it.

The room spun when he lifted her and settled into a rainbow of delight when he laid her on the big bed.

A thundering herd of elephants charged up the hall. Charlotte came awake and sat up before the stampede could trample her.

"Daddy, Daddy, Daddy," the twins chanted as they pounded on the door.

Falling back in relief, she turned her head slightly and met the twinkling eyes of her husband.

Charlotte knew heat flooded her cheeks—she could feel it—but she refused to look away. After his words of last night, she didn't care if he saw her shyness or embarrassment. After his loving touch and caresses, she didn't care much about anything except experiencing them again.

"Lottie, Lottie, Lottie."

The pounding became even louder.

"I think our daughters are awake," Asher said slowly, his hand coming to cup Lottie's cheek, his thumb tracing delicate paths on her skin.

"Are you sure there are only two little girls out there? It sounded more like a stampeding herd."

He laughed. "Get something on, and I'll let in the herd."

He rose and drew on a pair of pajama bottoms. Waiting only long enough for Charlotte to drop a nightgown over her head, he opened the door. The twins danced in, peeking around him to see Charlotte in the big bed. They made a beeline for her and clamored to get up.

Asher watched, unable to believe his life had changed so drastically the last few weeks.

Before leaving for Bangkok, he'd been for all intents and purposes a bachelor. Now he had a wife and two daughters. The feeling hit him hard. The realization a revelation.

He loved them.

All of them.

His gaze sought Charlotte's. No wonder he'd almost panicked last night when she said she didn't want shares. He feared she wanted to end their marriage. And he knew that he could never let her go. Not because she'd make the girls a wonderful mother.

He couldn't let her go because his life would be nothing without Charlotte Callahan in it!

"What?" she asked, smiling at something Kennedy had said. Slowly her smile began to fade. "Is something wrong?"

"I don't think so," Asher said.

For the first time in years, everything seemed perfect. He had a wife who loved him and his daughters. And he loved her. He envisioned their future. They'd build a strong bond, forged in love, not merely mutual interests as he'd once so arrogantly thought.

"I love you, Lottie," he said softly.

Her eyes flooded with tears as she gazed at him.

"Truly?"

"Lottie sad?" Kennedy said, snuggling closer.

"Mommy two," Madison said loudly, then patted Charlotte's arm. "Mommy two sad?"

"No, actually, I'm so happy I think I'll burst," Charlotte said as the tears ran down her cheeks.

Her gaze never wavered from Asher's.

He crossed the room and gathered her into a tight embrace, kissing her hard.

"Me, too, Daddy, kiss me, too," Kennedy said, pushing against him.

"Tonight, we'll see if Jennifer can stay and we'll go to dinner. We need some time alone."

She nodded, clutching his shoulder as if she'd never let go.

"Marco's, where there's dancing," Asher said.

"Sounds great."

"Then we'll come home and these two will be asleep and we can—"

Her fingers covered his mouth.

"I know exactly what we can do. Do you really love me?"

"With all my heart. I realized it when I saw you this morning with the twins. I love them so much, and then I realized I loved you as much—differently, but every bit as strong."

"That's why I married you, you know," she said softly. "I knew when you asked me in the meadow that I loved you. I was slow in responding, and you rushed in with the offer of shares. Haven't you told us at work never to rush negotiations?"

He smiled, shifted slightly to accommodate the two little girls who wanted to be included in his arms.

"I couldn't take the chance you'd say no. And I don't want you to say no to my next suggestion."

"The way I feel right now, I doubt I could deny you anything," she said, smiling radiantly.

"Keep the shares. Learn as you go with the company. I can't have my wife working for a competitor. Remember, Addie and I were about your age when we started out. We didn't know that much but learned as we went along. Stay, Lottie. Stay and build Callahan Associates with me and the girls."

"Do you think I should?" she asked.

"Absolutely."

He leaned forward to kiss her again.

"I can't believe it. I wish we had told each other this a week ago. Do you realize this is the first-week anniversary of our wedding?"

"As soon as we can get things straight at work, we'll take off for a real honeymoon. Just the two of us."

"I thought you married me to watch these two."

She indicated the squirming girls.

"That's the reason I told you. Sooner or later Sarah would

have found someone who could live in. I may even have thought that was the reason for a few days. But this last week has proved I want more than a nanny. I want you, for yourself, because I love you. Forever."

She hugged him tightly.

"I love you, Asher. I will forever."

"Hug me, Mommy," Madison demanded, not to be slighted.

"Me, too," said Kennedy.

"Oh, my precious daughters. I love you both almost as much as I love your daddy."

She gathered them in for a sweet hug, her eyes seeking Asher's. "We're going to have the most amazing life together! I can't wait to see all that happens.

If you enjoyed **Love Times Three**,
please consider leaving a review.

More books by Barbara McMahon

Golden Gate Romance Series
Billionaire's Betrothal
Dakota's Hero
Finding a Wife for Tanner
Love Times Three
Unexpected Encounter
Boss's Baby
A Special Kiss

Cowboys of Wildcat Creek
Valentine's Cowboy Rescue
Shelly and the Cowboy
Kristi's Cowboy Hero
Holly's Reluctant Cowboy
A Cowboy for Eliza

Sweet Reunion Romance Collection
Unexpected Reunion
Unpredictable Reunion
Unanticipated Reunion

The Talmadge Sisters
Letters to Caroline
Michelle's Marriage Deal
Trusting Abby

The Harts of Texas Series
Rebel Heart
Tangled Hearts
Reckless Heart

A Sweet Clean Christmas Romance Collection
The Christmas Cop
The Cowboy's Special Christmas
A Soldier's Christmas
A Teaspoon of Mistletoe
The Christmas Locket
A Key West Christmas

Cowboy Heroes Series
Blue Bells on the Hill
Cowboy's Bride
One Stubborn Cowboy
Crazy About a Cowboy
Never Doubt a Cowboy
Cowboy Marshal
Summer Cowboy
Second Chance Cowboy
Movie Star Cowboy

Tropical Escape Series
Island Rendezvous
Come into the Sun
Island Paradise

Rocky Point Series
Rocky Point Legacy
Rocky Point Reunion
Rocky Point Promise
Rocky Point Hero
Rocky Point Inn
Rocky Point Dawn

The Ultimate Billionaires
The Cynical Sheikh
Falling for the Sheikh
A Sheikh of Her Own
The Unforgettable Sheikh

Sweet Romance Stand-alone Collection
Because of You
Cowboy Charade
I'll Take Forever
Jared's Promise
Mail Order Bride
Not Really Married
Sweet Meant To Be
The Cowboy Comes Home
The Paper Marriage
Trusting Jake
The Banished Bride